Elven Roots

Forging the Future

Elven Roots Book 3

Jennifer Abrahamsen

ISBN: 979-8-9899852-7-2

Cover Art by Darren C. Leonard

Printed in the United States of America

This book is dedicated to my nephew, Landon.

PROLOGUE

Skilanis entered the small cottage behind the slave quarters. There were twenty females seated on the floor, each grinding bone to dust in a bowl with a pestle, and an older female sitting at a table off to the right.

"Good day, Master," the old elf greeted Skilanis. "We have quite a haul for you."

"I am happy to hear it."

Skilanis often used the powder created in this hut to pull beings from Niflheim into Alfheim. The bones came from humans with Elven blood.

"The supply of bones has dwindled," Skilanis continued. "Precision strikes on those with Elven blood are no longer feasible since the death of most of the Elite Draw. Your days of grinding bone are at an end."

Skilanis retreated from the cottage carrying a jar of bone dust. He trusted no one to deliver this last batch to the cave deep within the Dredskog Forest. Unlike when drawing creatures from the realm of the dead, the latest batch of powder needed to be weighed precisely. None could be permitted to spill. Skilanis would carry the precious cargo himself and begin the last of his preparations. His ascent to the throne had been in the making for years. Skilanis had served under the self-proclaimed king of Dredfall since the kingdom had first been hewn out of Lillerem and it was now time for that king to fall.

He turned back to look at the cottage and briefly considered setting fire to it with the slave women inside. They were malnourished and frail. A quick death might be considered merciful. Skilanis's moment of weakness passed. He turned back toward the forest, deciding to let the women perish at their own pace.

A cataclysm would come. A World Destroyer from Muspelheim, the realm of fire, would bring it.

Leif swung his sword in an arc, aiming for his brother's head. Gunnar held Forsvarer before him, easily deflecting Leif's clumsy blow with his family's sword. Leif wobbled and reached out for the chair beside the window to maintain his balance. After taking the last pull of whiskey, Leif hurled the empty bottle toward Gunnar with his left hand. The bottle smashed into the wall over Gunnar's left shoulder. Leif charged forward, once again raising his sword, but Gunnar sidestepped deftly. As Leif's bumbling form moved by, Gunnar stuck out his foot and tripped his brother. Leif followed his recently thrown bottle into the wall behind Gunnar.

Joral quickly moved to tie Leif's hands and feet. Gunnar rolled Leif's unconscious form over and picked a shard of glass from his forehead.

"I wish it didn't need to be this way," said Joral.

"Leif never makes things easy. Now that Bane secured that tincture from Trego, Leif can have the best of both worlds. He can help us save his daughter while still avoiding the emotional pain he has been drowning with alcohol in the human realm," lamented Gunnar.

"I know," said Joral. "It just feels wrong to force him to do the right thing."

"I've learned you can't win when it comes to Leif," replied Gunnar. "If we let him stay here in his own world of self-pity, he will regret letting his daughter rot in the hands of the King of Dredfall. It will cause him to spiral farther into the darkness, and even worse, it might cause us to be unable to free Kindra. On the other hand, you are currently seeing the direct result of forcing Leif to participate in this rescue."

"I just hope Bane has that concoction mixed, and it is ready for Leif to drink when we drag him into Alfheim. Facing Leif in the human realm while he is drunk is entirely different from fighting him, sober and in a rage, on the other side of the portal. Now, help me carry him down the steps."

Alek dumped a mixture of venison and ground cartilage into large metal bowls. The venison was leftover cuts from the butcher and a substantial amount of innards, usually reserved for compost. Alek had learned the cartilage provided essential minerals, as well as the thicker consistency required of the mushy meal to simulate a fresh kill and encourage the beasts to feed. The bloody concoction made his stomach churn. Holding his breath as long and as often as he could, Alek delivered dinner to each of the dark creatures kept in this area. Alek was unsure how the Master procured these beings, but he knew none of them originated in Alfheim. The beasts in these cages were only found in the darker realms.

While he waited for the bowls to be licked clean, Alek prepared a few smaller servings for the actual hounds King Ulford kept at the kennel. This was the job Alek had been enlisted for as a young elf at age twenty. Because of the slow nature by which elves age, Alek had only just learned to lace up his boots and prepare his own meals. If Alek had not been a slave, he would have started school at that age instead of going off to work in the kennels. He had been preparing meals for Ulford's hunting dogs for eighteen years now. The addition of the Master's creatures to the kennels had started half that time ago, and Alek was still very uncomfortable around them.

On his way to feed the dogs, Alek passed one of the Master's pets. Unlike the hounds which were working dogs and only used for hunts, and unlike the grotesque creatures Alek had just fed, the Master's pets roamed the kennels freely. They resembled dogs, but were more than double Alek's size. When Alek looked the creatures in the eyes, there was no mistake that these were not canines. Alek felt as if the animals were analyzing him, and he shuddered involuntarily. Alek steeled himself as he walked by one. He gave it a pat on the head, as he often did to show the creatures he was not a threat. The damn things used the place like an inn. They came and went as they pleased and most only dropped by to take a nap where it was dry.

Alek was still watching the hairy animal lope toward the exit when a shadow fell over him. The imposing form of the Master filled the doorway. He carried one side of a large canvas bag. Tobias, the houndsman, came through the doorway holding the other end of the sack. Alek backed up against the wall so the two males could squeeze by with their cargo. Just before turning the corner, the Master looked back at Alek.

"You, slave! How would you like a promotion? Come this way."

At first Alek didn't respond. This was an opportunity to prove his worth, and Alek willed his body to move forward, but he was rooted to the spot. Though this could be Alek's chance for advancement, a false move under the Master's watchful eye would be dangerous. Alek took a breath and released it slowly, then followed the men to an open cell. They unzipped the canvas bag and rolled a female form from inside it. Tobias dragged the female by her arms into the cell, placing her on a thin layer of dry hay. Tobias stepped out of the cell, grabbed the duffel from the stone floor and walked off, presumably to check on the hounds. Alek, who was still holding the bowl intended for the canines, turned to follow behind him. The movement caught the Master's eye, and he looked at Alek as if he had finally remembered the young elf was standing in the corner.

"Make those the last bowls you deliver to the beasts and dogs of this kennel. I'm replacing your duties with a new task. You must guard this prisoner. Do not let her pretty face and smaller stature fool you. She is a powerful half-elf from the human realm. Care for her well, and remain vigilant! She may attempt to harm you or even try to escape. I will check in on her every few weeks to be sure you are performing your duties well. Now, give that slop to Ulford's hounds and get back here to begin your watch."

Alek, ecstatic over earning a promotion, trotted off immediately, responding to the Master with only a nod of his head. He was just naïve enough to believe the Master had assigned an elf, with no experience and not even old enough to shave, to guard a prisoner. Alek wound his way to the hounds' cages and arrived to find Tobias waiting for him. The male was making a good show of looking as if he had no interest in Alek, cleaning the cage of a very sweet female huntress named Daisy.

Alek delivered the metal dishes he had in his arms to their furry recipients and shook out his hands. His fingers were numb from holding the heavy bowls for so long. He pulled some dried meat from his pocket and gnawed on it casually to give the impression he was not dying for Tobias to ask what had occurred after he left. Elves of Alek's age were not known for patience, and it was a struggle for the boy to keep from bursting with his news.

Daisy was milking the attention Tobias afforded her for all she could, ducking under him as he reached in to clean her space so Tobias would have no choice but to run his hands over the sleek black-and-tan fur. Though Tobias continued to scrub the cage and pet the hound, Alek could feel the male's eyes on him. "Well... what did the Master want from you?" Tobias finally gave in and asked.

Alek, thrilled with his new position, replied while still chewing the remains of his snack. "Unfortunately for you, Tobias, you'll be short-handed for a bit. I got me a new job. No more scrubbing muck out of these cages for me."

Tobias raised an eyebrow. "You sure that's a good thing? What will you be doing instead?"

Alek, his mouth now clear of food, puffed out his slim chest and crossed his arms. "The Master promoted me to guard duty. I get to sit around and make sure that prisoner you two brought in stays put."

"That sounds like an important job. Are you sure you're ready for something like that?" Tobias asked.

"It's not like she can get out of the cage," Alek said. "I'll just be sitting there watching her."

"I fear it might get a little boring," said Tobias. "You're going to have to sit outside that cell for hours with nothing to do but stare at the wall."

Alek allowed a moment to try to picture the new life his promotion offered. He conceded that the Master had likely described the position as 'guard duty' as a means to convince Alek to jump at the opportunity to become a full-time babysitter. Unlike the animals Alek currently cared for, this prisoner could talk and would likely have needs beyond a few bowls of bone meal throughout the day. His entire world would revolve around his prisoner.

Tobias, unaware Alek was still processing the last comment, continued. "There won't be any going back to the barracks with the other children and you won't have time to play any football."

Tobias's warning couldn't entirely rid the excitement from Alek's small body. He was no longer a child. They'd be moving him out of the barracks and chaining him up with the adult slaves soon enough. Alek was certain he could secure himself a position with a little more freedom if he served the Master well in this new task. Alek tamped down the temptation to ask what Tobias had done to get his job as houndsman. Surely, there was something that set Tobias apart from the other slaves. *Maybe he was just really good with hounds?*

"Sorry, Tobias. You ain't raining on my good fortune! We all gotta start somewhere and this is my chance. I'll make sure the Master knows he can trust me with the big jobs. If you need me, I'll be with the prisoner."

As usual, Alek spoke without thinking. His flippant reply to Tobias had felt right a moment ago, but the older elf's words replayed in Alek's mind shortly after Alek left the room. He wound back down the halls toward his newly assigned charge, thinking about football. Tobias's comment about missing out on the matches the children played needled him. Alek had not considered the things he would not get to do because of his new position. He had merely been excited to rid himself of canine waste and metal bowls of bloody venison meal. As he neared the prisoner's cage, he heard a female voice.

"Hey! Is there anyone out there?"

CHAPTER 1

Krish gave the signal. One long trill, followed by two short whistles. He moved forward from the edge of the forest. Gunnar and Joral were doing the same, each approaching the city from a different direction. Krish moved in a graceful crouch, watching the archers atop the wall. He safely reached the southern gate and hid himself among the bushes. There were only two guards posted outside of the gate to check the identification of anyone wishing to enter. At this time, there was not a line of people waiting to get in.

Fallholm was not exactly a vacation destination. As the capital city in the kingdom of Dredfall, a land ruled by a self-proclaimed king, it was not the type of stronghold people tried to break into. Most of the guards at the wall of this city faced inward to prevent the inhabitants from leaving. Almost sixty percent of the residents of the city inside this wall were slaves. Another twenty percent of the people who lived here served in the Dredfall army. Of the remaining twenty percent, some were merchants and tradespeople, but most comprised the families of the Dredfall soldiers.

Leif, a prince of Lillerem through the Great King Andril's line, came into view. Dressed as a vagrant, he stumbled down the road toward Krish's position. He was singing loudly and terribly off-key as he zig-zagged closer to the entrance to the city. The song was about five people going on some kind of boat excursion that was only supposed to take three hours. Krish shook his head. Having been raised in the human realm, Leif often spoke about objects or people for which Krish had little frame of reference. The song was unfamiliar to Krish and ridiculous, but Leif had likely chosen it for just that reason. It certainly was distracting. At first, it appeared one guard would hang back to maintain the security of the city gate, but Leif dropped his trousers a few inches and began urinating in the middle of the path. This was the spark the second guard needed to take action, and both guards moved forward from the city entrance to investigate the drunk staggering along the road. Leif shot Krish a wink as the guards drew closer to him and away from Krish. Krish shook his head in disgust as he entered the city.

Once inside, Krish straightened his posture and headed toward the outdoor market. It was one of the few places within Fallholm that was not used by the military. He made his way to the leather worker. She saw his approach, but continued hawking her wares. Krish ducked past her and into her enclosed carriage to join Joral and Gunnar, each a prince of Lillerem because they descended from King Blaith, the last King of Lillerem in its entirety. The stench that greeted him almost caused him to lose his breakfast. Joral was buttoning a clean shirt over newly donned trousers. Gunnar, shirtless, had yet to remove his filthy britches.

"I do not understand why it was you who were assigned the main gate as your entry point," groused Joral. "The sewers were dreadful and likely the inspiration for the naming of this forsaken kingdom."

"I am the Crown Prince of Lillerem. It would be unseemly for me to be crawling around in excrement. Besides, the level of detritus barely reached your waist if Gunnar's britches are any indication," replied Krish. "Now, finish getting out of those clothes and toss them out the back door. I'd like to avoid Frida's wrath over disgracing her merchant wagon with the stench."

Joral and Gunnar exchanged a look of shared irritation, but quickly finished changing. The trio exited the carriage through the door opposite the open market, depositing the soiled clothing on the side of the path as they headed toward Castle Bindrell. The stone façade of the structure remained from the time that the city had been part of the Kingdom of Lillerem, but the princes expected the interior of the castle would be reimagined since its razing at the time Ulford declared himself King of his newly formed territory of Dredfall.

The military presence grew as they left the bustle of the marketplace and moved closer to their destination. A soldier approached from the opposite direction. The chest plate of his uniform bore the red dagger piercing the sun. Ulford's sigil supposedly represented his ability to bleed the power of the sun and wield it against his enemies. Leif had once said the sun was actually a stone, and the sigil served as a reminder to Ulford that he could not pull blood from that stone with a dagger. Ulford kept his people in chains and demanded they work for the benefit of the Crown from dawn until well after the sun set below the horizon. He required more than the people could give, and most were dead before seeing eighty summers. That was the equivalent of a human dying of exhaustion around the age of twenty-five.

The soldier removed his helmet and bright red locks of hair fell to frame an inhumanly handsome face. This was no soldier of Dredfall. Leif's emerald eyes sparkled as he threw the princes a grin that had been known to melt females' hearts. He dropped a bag from his shoulders and began pulling cloth from within it. When Leif threw a bundle to Krish, it unfurled in the air to reveal itself as a Dredfall uniform.

"There were two guards at the gate. I figured the second uniform shouldn't go to waste, so I grabbed it for you," Leif said.

"I saw the two guards and was concerned for a moment there that you actually were drunk, somehow, and would fail to dispatch them," Krish replied.

"My body might prevent itself from feeling the assets of alcohol in this realm, but that drink Trego brews is magical! I enjoyed a little extra before setting out on the mission, but I was in control of myself by the time I approached the gate. The only effect that lingers is the absence of forethought and lack of regret for my actions."

Gunnar huffed. "You say that as if it were unusual."

Gunnar was only just beginning to understand his brother's complicated relationship with mind-altering substances. Leif spent the majority of his life in the human realm. This allowed him to feel the effects of the alcohol he used to drown out the depression and anxiety Leif battled in his mind. Of course, it also prevented him from being a functioning member of society. On the outside, Leif appeared to be self-centered, uncaring, and completely uninterested in the feelings of others. It was slowly becoming evident to Gunnar that these behaviors were a mechanism Leif used to prevent himself from feeling hurt and unworthy. Gunnar was often hard on his younger sibling, but no one was harder on Leif than Leif was.

Krish emerged from the tall reeds adjacent to the path, dressed as a second Dredfall soldier. He stuffed his own clothing into Leif's small pack and took the spot beside him as the group marched on as one. To distant eyes, it appeared as if two soldiers were leading thieves from the market to the prison below the castle. The group left the path and continued along the castle wall instead of going to the prison entrance, following the perimeter until they reached a wooden door. They stood beyond the entrance so that when it opened, the door would shield them from the view of anyone exiting.

"All the doors in this realm remind me of whiskey barrels," complained Leif. "Every one of them is oak with iron embellishments. It's as if even the doors know I need a drink."

The door opened and a slave, dressed in frayed trousers and little else, exited with a chamber pot in his hands. He propped the door with a rock and walked away from the castle. Joral drove the pommel of his sword into the back of the slave's head. Gunnar was moving to drag the limp form closer to the castle wall before the slave's body even fell to the ground. He leaned in close to be sure the slave was breathing before standing to join the others as they made their way into the castle.

"You did not need to hit him so hard," Gunnar reprimanded Joral.

"He will be fine. We need to be sure he remains out there until we've reached the throne room," replied Joral.

Not for the first time, Krish wondered if Ulford would even be in the throne room when the princes arrived. Unlike Lillerem's King, Ulford often left his castle to oversee the activity in his military camps. The princes were relying on Ulford being a creature of habit. Using the pretext of entering the city to sell her leather crafts, Frida had monitored Ulford's movements for the last two weeks. She was confident Ulford would take his breakfast in the throne room after he made his morning rounds. That time was reserved for free citizens of Fallholm to make any pleas to the King. Frida assured the princes it was unlikely there would be many civilians present while Ulford took his meal. Instead of addressing concerns, Ulford was better known for shackling those with complaints about the state of affairs.

The males ran through the passages, encountering handfuls of slaves, but no soldiers. Members of the First Draw would be waiting outside the doors leading to the throne room and within the room itself. The princes knew nearly all of them would be inexperienced. They would be replacements for the members of the draw who had never returned from their trip to the human realm. Jess, Kindra, and the princes had dispatched all members of the old guard except Imra and Skilanis.

Joral and Gunnar waited in the passage. Krish and Leif entered the main hall. The two strode directly to the two Elite Guards outside of the throne room. Five feet before the door, Leif teleported to a position behind the guard on the right and drew his dagger across the female's throat. The sound of the guard choking on her own blood caused the other guard to look over. Krish threw his dagger and caught that guard in the middle of his neck. He slumped silently to the floor, his spinal cord severed. Joral and Gunnar entered the hall and joined Krish and Leif outside of the throne room.

Gunnar pulled Forsvarer from its sheath and counted down quietly from three. Leif blinked out of sight and the other three princes charged through the doorway and into a mass of waiting Elite Guard members. The soldiers were poised for the fight, as if they had been waiting for the princes to arrive. Gunnar drove Forsvarer through the breastplate of the first guard to confront him. He spun to his left, pulling the sword free from his first victim and slicing it through the air and into the thigh of a second attacker. Blood sprayed and coated the floor, causing the next assailant to slip and land on his back. Gunnar impaled the guard with his family sword.

Leif had teleported himself into the room and worked his way to the left side. He reached out with the dagger in his left hand. When his target drew his hands up to block, Leif ran his sword through the soldier's gut. Pulling the sword from the first soldier's stomach, Leif flipped his dagger to hold it by the point. With his sword free, Leif hurled the dagger at a soldier on the other side of the room. It caught the guard between her eyes.

Joral sliced through bone and sinew, working his way to the raised dais at the front of the great hall. He halted and nearly lost his own head to the sword of an attacking guard as he stood paralyzed for just a moment. It wasn't Ulford on the throne.

Joral ducked the attack and swung his blade at his assailant's legs. The guard went down, and Joral quickly pierced the soldier's heart with the tip of his sword. Joral looked up at the throne again.

The person on the throne was not the evil, self-proclaimed king of Dredfall. A female occupied the throne. Dressed in a shimmering gold gown, the blonde lounged with her long legs over one arm of the throne and her back against the other. She dangled one heeled sandal from her big toe. Her face was so similar to Syndral's, Joral needed to remind himself that the person on the throne was not the ex-soldier of the Dredfall army who had helped defeat Ulford's assassins in the human realm. The female on the throne was Syndral's twin sister, Imra. Imra's build was less muscular than her sister's and she had a lithe silhouette. Where Syndral was built for power, Imra was built for speed and grace.

The head of the last Royal Guardsmen in the throne room rolled to Joral's feet. The other three princes came to stand beside Joral. Imra gracefully swiveled and brought her feet to the floor in front of the throne. Though Imra looked each of the princes over, from their toes to the tops of their heads, Joral couldn't help but feel as if her gaze lingered on his face. The scar that ran from his right eyebrow to his left cheek often drew people's attention, but Imra wore a look of pity, like none Joral had seen in the past. Imra was aware that it had been Joral's father, Ulford, the King of Dredfall, who had bestowed the scar.

Joral and Imra had met once before on an overgrown lot owned by Patty Tully, a human with Elven blood living in the human realm. Patty had kept a trailer there and Imra had been part of the party sent to kill her. Joral had not registered Imra's similarity to Syndral that day. Imra had not indicated she knew who Joral was, but even if she had known, she had not had time to study the scar on Joral's face during that first meeting. Cassidy, Jess's German Shepherd Dog, had launched himself at her. Imra had run for the fence and cleared it in several heartbeats. Joral and the others presumed Imra had immediately returned to Alfheim after the encounter because they had not seen or heard from her again.

"Joral, it has not been long enough," Imra said in a smoky voice.

"I'm surprised you stuck around until the end of the fight this time. Is it only dogs that frighten you?" asked Joral.

"You already know I am not a fighter. I was never supposed to come into contact with any of you while investigating the human realm on Ulford's behalf," said Imra. "The rest of the First Draw had their orders, but I was there looking for a deserter. Imagine my surprise when I learned my turncoat sister was working with the likes of you all."

Gunnar caught Joral's attention. He opened his eyes wide, silently reminding Joral that he needed to keep Imra talking. The princes had expected to find Ulford and Imra, together, in the throne room. The plan had been to end Ulford's existence, but to try not to harm Imra. It had been a last-minute promise to Syndral to keep her sister unscathed, if possible. With Ulford absent, the princes only knew that it was imperative to keep his seeress occupied here in the great hall, so she could not warn him of the other part of their plan.

Joral spoke again. "Where is your master?"

Imra giggled. "Master? You hold that male in higher regard than you realize. Ulford would be nothing without me. Did you really think I would not foresee your attack? I made sure he was out on the training grounds, surrounded by his soldiers. There is no way you will reach him today, or any other day."

Joral's heart skipped a beat. Perhaps she was already aware of the second half of the plan. Imra felt the future. She did not have visions, as one might expect of a seeress, but she sensed events that were going to happen. She intuitively knew when she needed to change her course of action to better her circumstances. Syndral had shared this knowledge about her sister and also that she thought Imra might use her power to help Ulford because she loved him.

Krish continued the stalling tactics. "If you knew we were coming, why did you stick around?"

"And miss the show? I've heard so much about the devastating effects of the combined power of the Princes of Lillerem. I wanted to see it in person. It's the only way I can be sure what we are up against. I noticed there was little magic used in this room today. Am I to believe that warriors as powerful as yourselves have nothing to wield but swords?"

Leif allowed the magic to build within him. His face remained serene, but the power begged for release. He permitted his magic to encircle Imra's throat, and he applied a little pressure.

"Ah! There it is. One of you is itching to show off. I have that effect on males," said Imra.

She gracefully stood from the throne and disappeared from sight.

"That was you, wasn't it, Leif?" Joral growled. "We were trying to keep her here. We were stalling to give Trego and Bane more time."

"Sorry," Leif replied flippantly. "I didn't get the memo. She was pissing me off. I was afraid I would want to kill her, and Syndral asked us not to do that."

"I didn't get the impression Imra was aware of what Trego and Bane are currently doing. Based on Syndral's theory that Imra can only feel a future that benefits her goals, I suspect that means Kindra's imprisonment was not an act to advance Ulford's cause," said Krish.

"Well, that's a good thing, right?" asked Leif.

Gunnar, often silent, spoke at last. "I am inclined to agree that Imra's ignorance is a sign that Ulford's plans do not rely on Kindra's captivity, but I am not sure that is a good thing. If Ulford isn't the one that is holding her, who is?"

CHAPTER 2

Alek sat on the floor of the library, digging through one last box of books. It wasn't really a library, but Alek liked to think of it as one. In reality, it was a large building with an open floor-plan. Stacked boxes of books created aisles that wound throughout the floor. Many of the piles held three or four boxes. The four-box stacks were taller than Alek. Alek loved the makeshift library, but not because of the words bound within the pages of the books. He enjoyed the time alone, without pressing chores. The books he was gathering were for Kindra. Alek checked the jumble of letters Kindra had written for him. He had accumulated a decent load of books with titles that matched most of the words on the paper.

It wasn't a challenging task. Alek spent much of his free time in the library, and he knew its layout well. Still, the young elf found the work laborious. Prior to his new job as a prison guard, Alek had mostly enjoyed the book warehouse because it was an excellent place to nap. The walk to and from the building had been relaxing. Alek found nothing relaxing about carrying books over that same distance. He stood up and bent to pick up the pile of books he was here procuring for his prisoner. He shook his unruly blond hair from his eyes and trudged back toward the castle.

When the Master ordered him to prisoner duty, Alek had been excited. The other slaves his age could keep mucking out stalls and digging trenches. It had been Alek's good fortune to watch the prisoner get dragged, unconscious, into a cage that day. Seeing the young elf watching from the corner with a bowl of food in his hands, the Master decided he would leave Alek to tend to the new resident. Alek could not wait to rid himself of the physical labor required by his kennel duty tasks and spend some time relaxing outside of the cages and watching his prisoner. The young elf had been unaware that his new duty would be grueling in a different way.

Early conversations with his prisoner had revealed to Alek that she was a princess. Maybe it was her position, or maybe she was just a bitch, but she seemed to think Alek was her personal servant. From the time she awoke and first called out to see if there was anyone there, she had been yelling for Alek every time she needed something. It wasn't once or twice a day either! Then again, it wasn't like Alek had anything else to absorb his time. Since taking on guard duty, he had missed several football matches. He had barely seen any of the other children, let alone played with them. They probably thought he had died.

At first, Alek thought the Elven princess he was charged with guarding was sending him on missions of no consequence, possibly so she would be free to plot an escape. It was only after his second trip to this library warehouse that it occurred to him that his prisoner might make her way out of the cell, but she would never slip past the hundespor that roamed freely in the kennels. There was no way Skilanis's pets would allow Kindra to leave. When Alek had first started work at the kennels, he thought he was expected to care for the hundespor, but he found they were more than capable of providing for themselves and only stayed in the kennels because they felt comfortable among the other beings that were ripped from their home realms by the Master.

Based on passages the princess read aloud from the books she had requested so far, Alek deduced that she was interested in studying royal genealogy. This made the chore of retrieving the information from the book warehouse even more tedious for Alek. He had absolutely no interest in anything or anyone of royal blood. Alek knew only two people descended from King Blaith, and he was not particularly fond of either of them. One of those people was the princess who kept sending him to the other side of Fallholm to retrieve books from the makeshift library. The other royal was the self-proclaimed king who had ordered the storage of all those books in that warehouse.

Alek was not an idiot. He might not have many summers behind him, but he understood how silly it would be to speak his distaste for King Ulford aloud. One of Alek's earliest memories was of Ulford pulling him from Mamma's skirts and putting him in a wagon with several other young elves. Some of those kids, Alek being one of them, were only just beginning to toddle around on two feet. Of course, Mamma had not tried to keep hold of the children. She wasn't really their mother, anyway. Mamma was an aging slave charged with caring for the youngest of the Elven children owned by Ulford. Once a slave was old enough to complete menial tasks, the child was removed from Mamma's care and placed in the barracks with the other young slaves.

Alek had never known his actual parents. No one had ever even attempted to feed him a story about them dying in a carriage accident when he was young. He only knew that Mamma had fed him and changed him, and then he went to the barracks. Some kids there remembered their families. They had come from Lindel or Lillerem when their parents were killed or captured. A few of the other children saw their parents now and again. Adult slaves were kept chained in cells, but there were times that the children glimpsed one of their parents working the fields.

Alek took the job as Kindra's guard with hope of avoiding a future as a shackled adult slave. Once Alek reached sixty summers, he would be removed from the barracks and chained up in the slave quarters at night, and then sent to the fields during the day. Alek was confident that giving up his relative freedom as an enslaved child to work as a guard would offer him the opportunity to secure a slave specialty job like the houndsman, Tobias, had somehow earned. Though Tobias was a slave, he had his own quarters and was treated similarly to the merchants, except he earned no coin for his duty.

Reaching Kindra's cell, Alek let himself in and plopped the stack of books he carried on the floor beside her. She did not look up from the manuscript in which she was engrossed. Alek missed the pleasant conversations he and Kindra had enjoyed in the first week of her imprisonment. The copper-haired princess had told Alek stories of adventure to pass the time. Alek learned she was a descendant of King Blaith, and therefore, also descended from King Andril. Since Blaith had been the king of Lillerem until its partition, Kindra was considered to be a princess of Lillerem. She told Alek she had saved

Castle Millspare in Aegroth from Ulford's army, and then she had sought out and defended humans with Elven blood in her own realm. Alek was confident the stories were embellished, but they were entertaining, so he kept his feelings to himself.

Alek had no inclination to defend Ulford. The man was Alek's owner. Alek, like all Dredfall residents, knew you couldn't trust people from Lillerem. Kindra was a special case, though. She was born in the human realm, and therefore not really a resident of Lillerem, and over the first week Alek grew more sympathetic to Kindra's cause. She was intent on destroying Ulford, Skilanis, and any who stood in her way. Skilanis, known as the Master among the slaves, was creepy. He surrounded himself with rotting creatures pulled from other realms. He was also responsible for keeping and organizing Ulford's slaves, whom he managed through fear and a heavy hand. Alek didn't hold any solid feelings about Ulford, but he would be happy to see Kindra remove Skilanis's head.

In his second week acting as Kindra's guard, Alek started becoming more convinced Skilanis might not remain Slave Master for much longer. Kindra had just finished telling a story about a journey to Gulentine Palace to complete research in the palace archives. She explained how Skilanis, Ulford, Imra and other members of the First Draw were all descendants of King Andril, and therefore all in line to inherit the throne of Lillerem. Alek had not absorbed the details, but he had been interested in how Ulford made it his mission to kill off every other living being that might stand in the way of his plans to conquer Lillerem. It meant there was a possibility Ulford might kill Skilanis before Kindra ever had the chance. That would suit Alek just fine.

It was then that Alek made his mistake. He had readily agreed to perform the small task of gathering some research materials to aid Kindra in discovering the existence of any children King Ulford may have fathered. Alek had jumped at the opportunity to visit the large warehouse where books and manuscripts were boxed up and stored when Ulford had deemed the Fallholm library to be an unnecessary drain on his coffers.

When Kindra requested Alek's help in ridding the realms of all those who were trying to hurt her and her family, Alek had come to a new realization. His new position may have been described to him as 'guarding the prisoner,' but his duties actually revolved around keeping the prisoner relatively happy and occupied. For whatever reason, the Master wanted the princess held prisoner, but did not wish her to be entirely uncomfortable. At times, Alek felt more like Kindra's servant than her guard. This was particularly irritating because the princess treated Alek like a child, even though they were about the same age. As an elf, Alek aged much slower than his human prisoner. Alek judged her to be in her late thirties while he had been alive for almost forty summers. There was a good chance Alek was actually older than Kindra, yet she bossed him around as if he were a younger sibling. Alek knew it wasn't about the years one had lived, though. He was a child, but he had seen a lot in his time and he wished Kindra would stop seeing him as she saw the students she worked with back home.

Though Alek enjoyed the trip to the library warehouse, Kindra had not stopped after sending him once, and Alek was beginning to loathe the almost daily trek. Sitting there in the cage with Kindra, Alek thought about the football match he was currently missing. Unlike the adult slaves, the children wore no chains. They stayed in the barracks at night and then completed chores, many of them labor intensive, during the day. As long as all assigned chores were complete, the slave children were relatively free.

With a sigh, he picked up a book he had just brought to Kindra and leafed through it. Alek's chore was never complete. He remained on guard duty day and night.

There were no pictures in the hardcover he had selected and the letters on the page didn't hold his attention. He closed the book and put it back on the pile.

At last, Kindra spoke. "If you are that bored, why don't you go see if you can scrounge up some food for us? Daylight is fading and the market will be closing down. It's a good time to work your magic."

It wasn't a terrible idea. Alek's stomach gave a brief rumble, as if to stoke him into action. He left Kindra's space and walked the halls of the kennels toward the exit. Darkness was indeed approaching. Alek knew this because the hundespor weren't milling about. Alek could understand why they preferred to hunt under the cover of darkness. It was less likely prey could see them. Stepping into the fresh air of the open market, located just to the right of the kennel entrance, Alek noted that most of the merchants were packing up for the day. Alek knew the fading light would hinder the sight of his own prey.

Many of the people selling and bartering in the market were actually owned by Ulford. They did not keep the day's earnings for themselves. Ulford liked the idea of a place where citizens could shop for their needs, but there were very few merchants who lived within the walls of Fallholm, and even fewer who cared to travel from outside of the city to hawk their wares. Ulford did not collect taxes from those selling within his city. Instead, he sent his slaves to sell the produce they cultivated and the goods they manufactured to compete directly with the other merchants. The slaves handed each day's earnings back to Ulford. Under threat of punishment from Master Skilanis, Ulford's slave merchants never attempted to keep a single coin.

Alek scurried past a table where a merchant was packing up different varieties of fruit. As Alek went, he slowed and closed his eyes for a moment. Concentrating, Alek floated two apples into the sack he kept beneath his tunic without ever using his hands. Next, Alek approached the table where someone was selling butterflied breast of chicken. The merchant here was not yet packing up. The two breasts that remained for sale would not keep until the following day, and the merchant was desperately trying to find buyers among the dwindling crowd.

"I'll offer half price," Alek said. He pulled his purse from his belt and held it in both hands between himself and the chicken merchant.

The older male scoffed. "Ten percent off, seeing how it's end of day."

"You only have one chicken remaining. Sell it to me at a deep discount and you can be home to your family within the hour," Alek argued.

"One left? Are you blind or are you —"

The merchant stopped speaking abruptly when he looked down at his table and saw there was only one remaining split breast. He looked ready to accuse Alek of theft when he saw both of Alek's hands were still clutching the coin purse. The merchant looked up and down the aisle, trying to glimpse the thief. There wasn't anyone hurrying away. The second chicken breast was in Alek's sack, tucked in with the apples. Alek had moved them there while the merchant's eyes had been on Alek's proffered coin purse.

Alek pretended not to notice any change in the table's display. "If you won't sell me your final chicken at half price, then I will get my dinner elsewhere."

"You do that, urchin," the merchant replied while still looking up and down the narrow street.

Alek turned and left the chicken table. Under the cover of the growing darkness, Alek transferred a handful of small cakes to his sack using his telekinesis. He was perfectly capable of stealing food without magic. One of the first survival skills he learned was how to steal food. After all, he was a slave child on the streets of an unkind city. Using his telekinesis to pilfer supper lessened the chances of being caught, though. As long as no one was paying close attention to Alek, he could usually take food from a table that was over five feet away.

Alek hurried back to the kennels with his haul. He and Kindra would eat well this evening. As Alek made his way through the entrance, the hounds were barking. They had eaten less than two hours prior, so Alek was curious about what else could get the canines so riled. He walked back to the area of the kennels where Ulford's hunting hounds were kept. Tobias, the houndsman, lay crumpled in the middle of the floor. Alek ran to the older male and checked to see if he was alive. Finding Tobias to be breathing, Alek hurried off to check on Kindra. He was supposed to be her prison guard, after all. If something happened to her, the Master would be sure Alek did not see tomorrow's sunrise.

Rounding the last turn before reaching Kindra's cell, Alek heard voices. An exceptionally deep male voice was speaking too low for Alek to make out the words. There was only one occupied cage in this dead-end hall. The deep voice must be someone speaking to Alek's prisoner. He backtracked to the little area where he sometimes sat alone, passing time while Kindra read. Alek moved behind the small table and two chairs to squat down in the shadows of a dark recess. He needed to know if the Master had sent someone to retrieve Kindra. If a messenger or soldier had arrived, and Alek had been absent, he was not just losing his job; he was soon to lose his life.

It wasn't long before an absolutely enormous male entered the space where Alek was hiding. He walked through the room quickly, taking long strides and not seeing Alek, and then he moved off toward the exit. Alek was happy he had resisted the urge to get up and follow the male when his prisoner entered the room with a willowy male, dressed in brightly colored clothing. The yellow of his tunic almost glowed in the darkness of the little room.

"Princess, it is imperative that we hurry. I regret you've missed your chance to bid farewell to the child, but it really shouldn't be a concern right now. I would think you would simply be grateful to be rid of this place."

Alek was not sure if the males taking his prisoner were here on behalf of Ulford, or the Master, but he understood that his charge was leaving the kennels. There was nothing keeping him here now, and it would not be long before the Master knew Alek had been derelict in his duty. As Kindra and the tall, thin male followed the same path the larger male had taken, Alek joined the march. He followed closely and silently behind the others. He exited the kennels and watched the larger male open the door to one of the nearby merchant wagons. Kindra and the two males entered the carriage, and it began moving immediately.

Alek ran to catch the wagon. As an afterthought, he used his magic to guide a blanket from the back of a nearby horse to his hands as he raised himself to the top of the wagon. He lay down and completely covered himself with the dark blanket. Alek hoped his lumpy shape would be invisible to the few soldiers stationed on the walls above as long as he kept still.

Alek could hear the sounds of several other wagons moving to join the one on which he was riding. He knew these were the carts and wagons of the few merchants who traveled from outside of Fallholm to peddle their food and wares. If he remained where he was, and no one spotted him, Alek was about to leave the city that he had called home for as long as he could remember.

Alek pressed his ear to the wood below his head. There were no voices coming from within the wagon. He really wanted to wriggle toward the front and take a peek over the edge to see who the driver was, but he couldn't risk being caught now. It did not matter anyway. If he was caught, he would be killed. The driver would accuse him of being a thief, and that was punishable by death. Ulford would brand him a runaway, and that would also bring a punishment of death. Skilanis had assigned him to guard a prisoner, and Alek had been absent when that prisoner left the kennels. Though Alek didn't know the exact consequence allotted for that transgression, since it was not as if there was a 'make-shift prison guard handbook', he was certain it would end in death as well. Any time the Master was angry, it ended in the death of a slave. All Alek could do right now was not get caught.

Alek remained motionless as his wagon approached the checkpoint. Only one wagon could pass through at a time and the drivers would need to stop and check out with the guards. Alek felt the wagon roll to a halt. They must have reached the gates.

"Evening, Miss Frida. How were sales today?"

"The usual," responded Alek's driver. "Just good enough to keep me coming back. I suppose you need to have a look in the back?"

"Rules are rules, but let's make it quick. I'm the only one on duty. The two guards who were supposed to be here at the gate deserted today. Took off without a word."

"I can't imagine they'll get far," Frida said. The wagon rocked as she climbed down from the box up front. "The forest beasts will take care of them if they try to make it to the border, and they'll be killed by their former brethren if they stay in Dredfall. I can't imagine any soldier leaving here. King Ulford provides well for you lot."

The door to the carriage creaked open, and the soldier replied, "Indeed he does. I'd never leave my post. I earn more coin—gods, Frida! Every time I check this wagon, it's even more of a mess!"

"Yeah, sorry about that. I really don't have a chance to tidy up until the end of the week. I just throw everything in at the close of each day."

The guard chuckled and Alek heard the door to the wagon close again. He was sure he had seen the two males and Kindra enter this wagon. *The interior must be extremely cluttered to hide three people so completely.* Alek had an itch on the back of his leg. It needed to be scratched. What if it was some kind of biting insect crawling on him and he was just letting it move over his skin? Alek quietly maneuvered his hand to the place that itched and pressed it into his leg. There did not seem to be anything beneath his pant leg. He grabbed the fabric between his thumb and forefinger and used the rough cloth to scratch his skin.

Frida climbed back up onto the box. Alek heard the reins smack against the backs of her two horses and the cart started to move again. Knowing the guards posted on the wall above the gate had a clear view of the top of the wagon, Alek held still. The path would meet a wider road just as the wagon left the sight of the guards posted on the wall. Alek had been up on the wall on two occasions. Both times, he had been sent to take a message to the guards posted above the gate. On his second trip to the wall, Alek had watched a wagon turn to the left in the distance before disappearing from view. The soldier had made a grand show of sealing the reply with wax so Alek would know the reply was not meant for prying eyes. Alek hadn't bothered telling the male that no one had ever taught him to read.

Alek was surprised when the wagon turned right where the path to the castle intersected with the road, because there were very few villages in this direction. Most people did not like to live so near the forest, as it was well known throughout Dredfall that Skilanis's pets left Fallholm each evening to hunt in those woods. Alek pulled the blanket from over his head and watched the tree limbs block out the moon and the stars at brief intervals. He breathed the crisp air and started to relax. For the first time since Alek had started making memories, he was outside of the city of Fallholm. The sounds of the horses' hooves and the creaking wagon started to put him to sleep.

CHAPTER 3

Alek startled from near sleep when the wagon veered off the road about ten minutes after making the turn from the castle path. Frida drove it a little way into the trees and pulled to a stop. She thumped twice on the boards of the cart behind her. Doors on either side of the wagon burst open and the wagon rocked violently. The sound of heavy items hitting the earth outside of the wagon told Alek that the wagon would probably be less cluttered in a moment.

"I really was beginning to think I would suffocate in there!" Alek recognized Kindra's voice.

An unfamiliar male voice replied, "Relax, princess. Bane will have all this extra stuff out of the wagon shortly."

The sound of heavy objects hitting the ground continued.

A deep voice Alek recognized from his final visit to the kennels said, "It would be much faster if one of you royal pains in the arse felt the desire to help."

"I feel no such thing, but I'm sure this won't take long," replied the unknown voice.

A moment later, the deep voice came again. "You can all load back up. There is now room for everyone to breathe."

Alek lost count of how many times the wagon rocked as the passengers re-entered. *How many people are crammed into this thing? The deep-voiced traveler, the new male I just heard, the one in the fancy clothes and Kindra are only four people. This thing rocked far too many times for four people.*

Frida bumped the cart back out onto the road and the horses pulled it steadily away from Fallholm. There was no need for silence anymore, and Alek could hear much of the conversation coming from within the wagon. Based on the voices, there were seven people riding inside and each filled the others in on various parts of the journey. Alek learned that Joral and Gunnar had entered the city through the sewer system. Alek had been in that sewer before. One of Ulford's hounds had tracked something deep into the sewer tunnels and didn't come back out. Tobias had claimed he was too large to fit through the tunnels and had sent Alek to retrieve the hound. Alek found the dog taking a nap below the center of the city. It had taken six hours and Alek would never forget the smell that had clung to his skin for a week after the ordeal.

Continuing to eavesdrop, Alek learned the lithe male with the fancy clothes was named Trego. Of all the wagon's passengers, he sounded like he was born to the highest station. He also had an accent that Alek had never heard before. All that meant was that Trego was not from Dredfall, Lillerem, or Nalahem, because Alek had only ever known people from those kingdoms. Trego was mixing some kind of drug that a male named Leif was desperate to have. Leif used language that could rival the toughest street thugs Alek had ever met. Both Leif's demands for the drug, and the language he used for those demands, were an evident source of irritation for Trego. Leif colorfully reminded Trego that the only reason Leif was still in Alfheim was because the drug Trego was mixing for him kept him in 'a perfect state of oblivion while still being able to fight with a sword'.

It only took a few minutes of conversation before Alek realized he recognized these people's names from Kindra's tales. Most of those stories had bored Alek, and he had only casually listened to the interesting ones. Alek really had not cared how each of them fit into the royal family tree. He did recall that Leif was Kindra's father and the language spewing from the male's mouth confirmed Kindra's description of his being 'a little rough around the edges and kind of a jerk.' Alek knew Gunnar, Joral and Bane were princes, but he couldn't recall how they were related to Kindra. Alek found he knew more details about Trego than most of the others. Trego was an extremely powerful healer. Alek remembered Kindra's story about him at Gulentine Palace because Trego had saved the life of a dog named Butch. Alek really liked the dogs at the kennels and he had hung on every word of the story about the dog getting stabbed while protecting Kindra, and the healer saving its life.

Alek listened for the nighttime rhythm of frogs belching and peeping outside of the wagon. He enjoyed those sounds and the way they always relaxed him to sleep at night. The issue right now, was that there were no sounds outside of the horses' clopping hooves and the wagon creaking. The wagon noises were not loud enough to drown out the sounds Alek longed to hear, though. Disconcertingly, there simply were no sounds of the night.

Kindra stared out through the wagon's small rear window. There was nothing to look at. It was all blackness. Prior to her imprisonment, Kindra had never been to Dredfall. She knew from the maps at Millspare that there were a few small villages between Fallholm and the Dredskog. The Dredskog was a dense forest running along the border of Dredfall and Lillerem. Alek had shared some stories about slaves running away and never returning. Her young guard insisted that the Dredskog was the reason Skilanis did not need to dispatch soldiers to locate the runaways. Alek, having worked in the kennels for years, knew exactly what kinds of creatures Skilanis sent after runaway slaves.

Slave or not, no person who entered the Dredskog after the sun set below the horizon could expect to avoid the hundespor that hunted the forest nightly. Bane and Joral were two former slaves who had defied the odds. They did not speak often of the harrowing journey they made together through the forest when they were just boys, but they had survived. It was difficult for Kindra to imagine the princes had ever been boys. They were not just any boys, either. They were both Ulford's sons. Bane's mother had been a slave and Joral's mother had been Ulford's wife, but both boys had been sent to live at the slave barracks. Bane was sent there after his birth, but Joral had lived within the walls of Castle Bindrell until his mother's death. Kindra looked over at the princes now. Neither male showed any outward signs of concern as the wagon wound through the last village before they would enter the Dredskog.

Frida brought the wagon to a halt outside of an inn in the center of the village. She banged on the wall of the wagon.

"Last call for personal needs and libations!" she called, loud enough for her passengers to hear.

Krish stepped from the wagon and held his hand out. Kindra took Krish's hand and allowed him to help her down the thin steps. The handsome male, with hair so blond it was nearly white, flashed her a huge smile. It felt good to hold Krish's hand, but Kindra was aware she had not showered in weeks and she was concerned she was currently offending the Crown Prince of Lillerem with her presence. Though Krish was her fiancé and should only be concerned that Kindra was safe, he had that aura of propriety that came from being raised in a palace.

"I missed you," Krish whispered as she exited the wagon. "You look beautiful, despite the coating of dirt you have accumulated."

"Thank you, I think?" Kindra replied.

"I know you've heard me say this before, but this time I really thought I'd lost you," said Krish.

Kindra turned to look into her prince's eyes. "It does seem we spend a considerable amount of time fearing one of us might not survive. Hopefully, this will be over soon and we can simply enjoy each other's company without all the added worry."

"Indeed," said Krish and he pecked her on the cheek.

Krish released Kindra's hand as she continued toward the inn. They had needed to keep quiet for about fifteen minutes after Kindra had entered the wagon, and she had not told Krish that she had missed him either, but she had expected... something. This was the first time they had been out of earshot of the others, but it wasn't like their relationship was a secret. As she walked up the three steps to the inn, Kindra pushed all the negative thoughts about her future husband aside. She turned at the top of the stairs and offered Krish a smile. She waited for him to join her and they entered the inn together. Krish immediately found the innkeeper to inquire about a warm bath for Kindra.

Leif, Joral, and Bane stood outside of the inn. Leif turned his back to the road, untied his trousers and urinated into the bushes in front of the inn. Joral looked up at the sky and shook his head.

"Care to join me back in the wagon, Bane? I don't know about you, but my legs are sufficiently stretched."

Both males walked back to Frida's cart, leaving Leif to his business in the bushes. Before they could climb back into the wagon, Gunnar exited and joined them.

"We should not remain here long. Did Krish give any indication of when we will depart from here?"

Both Joral and Bane shook their heads and Joral looked as if he was about to speak when Leif pushed past the group of warriors. He attempted to continue on through the door of the merchant cart, but Gunnar grabbed the back of his shirt and pulled him off the steps.

"You don't need any more of that mushroom brew Trego gives you. We'll be entering the Dredskog within the hour. There is no doubt your sword will be needed if we are to make it through the forest and arrive in Lillerem safely," said Gunnar.

"Is that what you think of me?" Leif asked. "You think the only force that drives me is the quest for a substance to separate my thoughts from reality?"

Leif pushed past his brother, shouldering Gunnar as he went. Gunnar shook his head and found Joral's eyes with his own. Joral clapped Gunnar on the shoulder as if to offer his apologies that Gunnar was saddled with Leif as a younger sibling.

"You know, you might want to consider just letting him do his own thing. Sometimes, I think he acts out just to spite you and your level-headed suggestions," Joral said to Gunnar.

"I've learned to pick my battles, believe me. When the battle ahead is anything but metaphorical, I refuse to hold my tongue. If he isn't able to function, he puts all of our lives at risk."

"He's your brother," said Joral. "I trust you when it comes to keeping him under control. If he wasn't the most powerful elf currently alive, I'd have suggested you leave him back in the human realm. I am well aware that our lives are safer with him here, but I feel even safer when Leif is sober."

Gunnar turned to address Bane as well and redirected the conversation. "Speaking of battles ahead, are you two ready for this?"

Bane grunted. Gunnar was not sure if it was an affirmation or a show of indifference, but at least the quiet warrior had responded. Joral was slowly shaking his head and Gunnar understood Joral was as uncertain as Bane had seemed sure.

"It has been so many summers since my last trip through the Dredskog. I shouldn't be alive. Bane and I were just children when we met the horrors of that forest. I'd be lying if I told you I was ready to do it again," admitted Joral.

"You said it yourself," Gunnar replied. "You were young. I will not pretend this trip will be easy, but I hope the nightmares we face as adults will look different from the way they did through the eyes of children."

"We had help, you know? I'm not sure that I ever told you that," said Joral. "There was an old lady. The older I get, the less sure I am about her being real, though. She popped up out of nowhere at least twice. Each time, Bane and I were near death. I don't know… it was so long ago. Maybe we imagined her."

"As I said," Gunnar replied uncomfortably, "things will probably look different now that you are older."

Joral did not look reassured as he turned and entered the merchant cart. Bane took a seat on the wheel of the wagon and began running a whetstone along the edge of his sword. Though Bane's face looked exactly the same as it always did, Gunnar felt the gargantuan warrior was likely concerned about the next part of the journey as well. Gunnar climbed up onto the box at the front of the wagon, where Frida sat with her hat pulled down over her eyes.

"At least Bane and Joral are taking the forest seriously," Gunnar said instead of greeting Frida. "You know, they made their way through the Dredskog when they had seen barely forty summers? It amazes me. That forest swallows warriors and hunters, but two kids, not even old enough to shave, managed to escape Dredfall and make it through the forest to Lillerem."

"How did they do it?" Frida asked, without raising her hat from her eyes. "All they ever say is that it was due to the kindness of strangers."

"You'll have to ask them," Gunnar replied. "I'm just hoping we have equally good fortune tonight. Do you think it would be better if we stayed here in the inn tonight and struck out in the morning?"

"The trip through the Dredskog will take more than a day. It doesn't matter if we leave now, or leave in the morning. We will still find ourselves in the forest at night."

Frida tilted her hat back on her head so she could meet Gunnar's gaze. She could see the worry behind his stoic features. Frida had known Gunnar for a very long time. They had not spoken to each other for thirty-nine years, but he had not changed at all. The male always appeared impassive, but he was more like Leif than one might realize. Emotions roiled beneath Gunnar's calm exterior. One could see them, but only if you caught the fleeting change in his facial expressions.

"It must have been the Little Folk," said Frida.

Gunnar was surprised. It was unlike Frida to offer an answer that was more spiritual than practical. He was unsure if she was only trying to lighten the mood.

"That must be how Bane and Joral made it through the Dredskog. I know there are those who tell of miraculous survivals because of the aid provided by the Little Folk. I have no evidence those tales are true, but I have seen the Little Folk in the forest south of Smalgroth," replied Gunnar.

"You're lucky. There are not many who even know they are there," replied Frida.

"Ha!" Gunnar laughed loudly. "I hear them rustling underfoot often and I've seen them on more than one occasion. When we traveled through Smalgroth to Gulentine Palace, the Little Folk had a fun time torturing Jess's dog, Butch."

"That poor dog has been through so much. What did the little devils do to him?" asked Frida.

"As we walked the trail through the trees, the Little Folk would wait until Butch wasn't paying attention, then they would reach out from the bushes with a twig and whack him on the nose, or his foot. The poor dog was hopping back and forth, wondering where the next attack would come from. On the way home to Millspare, Butch didn't even want to enter the forest."

"That's terrible!" Frida cried, but she was laughing.

Frida tilted her hat back down over her eyes. She was going to need to catch a little nap before their impending forest adventure. Gunnar sat next to her in silence, enjoying the chance to be near the person he hadn't realized he had missed having in his life.

On the roof of the wagon, Alek was nearly in tears. His bladder was so full he was convinced he was leaking urine into his britches. He had hoped the entire group would go inside the inn and use the facilities or enjoy a meal. Not only had most of them remained outside, but three of them were not even in the wagon. If Alek moved, he would be heard. He was out of options and was convinced he would need to relieve himself while lying here on the roof.

The wagon rocked and Bane let out a grunt as he pushed his weight off the wheel he had been using as a seat and then entered the wagon. Alek silently levitated from the roof of the wagon and lowered himself to the ground at the rear of the cart. He walked a short distance from the wagon and started untying his britches before he even found his way behind a row of barrels. He was mid-stream when Kindra and Krish exited the inn and walked straight to the wagon. Kindra was still wearing the same tattered clothes, but she had washed up. The skin that could be seen was clean and her hair was neatly braided.

Alek had to make a decision. He could stay here, in this small village, and hope Skilanis did not attempt to find him, or he could make a run for it and get back up onto the roof of the merchant cart to continue his adventure toward the unknown. Kindra had already climbed up into the wagon and Krish was entering through the doorway. The wheels started to turn. As soon as Alek was finished relieving himself, he broke into a run. Glancing to the left and right, he saw no one in the streets and lifted himself back to the top of the wagon. This was his only chance to escape the Kingdom of Dredfall and discover a new life.

Alek removed an apple from the sack he still had tucked in his tunic. The sound of the wheels on the road and creaking of the wagon hid the crunching of the fruit in his mouth. Alek tried to imagine what he was going to say when the wagon reached Lillerem and he was inevitably discovered. He really didn't think anyone traveling in this party would take issue with him hitching a ride. He imagined climbing quietly from the wagon at the first stop after leaving the Dredskog. If Kindra saw him, Alek would admit to stowing away atop the cart and thank the group for the accidental rescue.

The dark night grew even darker as the wagon rolled into the edge of the forest. Alek found it peaceful. The pine needles on the ground deadened the sound of the wagon's wheels pounding the earth. Alek lay back and closed his eyes. Listening to the nighttime sounds, Alek was rocked to sleep by the motion of the wagon and thoughts of what freedom would taste like in the Kingdom to the south.

CHAPTER 4

Alek's eyes popped open. The wagon wasn't moving. There were grunts and shouts coming from all around him. It was a testament to how little sleep used to get in the kennels that he had not woken up before now. Swords were clanging and there were unnatural growls and squeals. Alek crawled to the edge of the roof and peered over the side. Almost directly below him, Gunnar and Joral stood back to back, moving in a circle, swords swirling through the air. Alek recognized the otherworldly creatures they were fighting. These were Skilanis's monsters. Alek could see at least two different varieties.

Joral's sword removed the head of a frost giant with white skin and ice-blue eyes. Alek knew from feeding and watering creatures like these in the kennels that they preferred the cold. Though the forest was nippy, and the attacking monsters had brought even more of a chill with them, it was still far too warm for them here. They were slow, almost lumbering, in this climate. Gunnar and Joral were cutting them down easily, even in such large numbers.

Closer to the front of the wagon, Bane fought against langen dropping from the trees. The snake-like creatures had no arms or legs. They had gray fur instead of the scales one would see on a snake, and their eyes glowed red. For a hulking beast of an elf, Bane was skilled with his sword and lightning-quick. The creatures were not even hitting the ground before Bane sliced through them with his blade. A langen landed on Bane's back and started curling around his neck. Bane wrenched the creature from its perch and threw it to the ground. He stomped on the langen's head with a giant black boot.

Alek crept to the other side of the wagon's roof. Here, Alek could see Kindra standing with her back to the doorway, hands out before her. She was using magic to hold off a hoard of lumbering, icy creatures. Krish moved among them with his blade. Alek was mesmerized by the Crown Prince. The grace and confidence emanating from the male distracted Alek to where he almost missed the much greater threat hovering just outside of the surrounding chaos. Alek sniffed the air. He inhaled the potent scent of rotting mushrooms.

Alek opened his mouth to shout a warning, but someone grabbed him by the back of the neck and hauled him to his feet. Alek was staring at a broad, well-muscled chest. The male in front of him wore no shirt. Alek slowly raised his head to look up at the face of his captor. The warrior's straight red hair hung in his face, but did nothing to hide his bright emerald eyes. The color was unnatural. Still, the resemblance to Kindra was unmistakable. Leif stared back at Alek with one eyebrow raised and the corner of his mouth turned up.

"What the hell do we have here?" asked Leif.

The words started tumbling from Alek's mouth. "You're Leif, Kindra's father. I'm Alek. I'm her... well, I was her guard at the kennel. The Master... Skilanis would have killed me for letting her get away, so I ran. Listen, you need to warn them. Smell the air."

"You listen, Alek, is it? All I smell are the mushrooms from the forest floor," began Leif.

Alek interrupted. "You don't think it's strange that you can smell the mushrooms so strongly?"

Leif, still holding Alek's shirt in a death-grip, took a deep breath. The smell of mushrooms was incredibly strong. Krish and Gunnar had mentioned mushrooms months ago. Mist creatures had attacked them outside of Castle Millspare, and the smell of mushrooms had been the only warning they had noticed.

Leif released Alek. "Mist creatures!" he screamed as he leaped from the top of the wagon.

Alek knew them as merknifol, but he supposed 'mist creature' summed them up well. The humanoid forms did not walk or run; they skated over land, seeming to float. They were invisible until they decided to be seen. The creatures preferred to lurk within the darkness. A weaponless traveler would find themselves prey to the merknifol, seconds after one showed itself, if the traveler had not noticed the premonitory scent of mushrooms. The creatures were known to approach campers and leach their souls as they slept. For a group of armed travelers, such as those Alek had joined, the merknifol were relatively easy to kill. Any blow from a blade or puncture from an arrow turned the creatures into the same mist they liked to hide within. The trick was to keep them from touching you first.

Alek watched the fight below. Spinning on the wagon's roof, he had a view of the battle on all sides. If the Master has sent merknifol as well as frost giants and langen, then he had likely sent other terrors after the escaped princess as well. It was also evident that the sheer number of gruesome creatures surrounding the wagon would take time to defeat. There would likely be injuries.

Alek looked over the front of the merchant wagon's roof. Frida still struggled with the reins and spoke soothing words to the horses.

"Excuse me, Frida?"

The female attempted to look over her shoulder while still holding onto the horses.

"I'm a little busy!" she yelled back. "Who are you, and why are you on the roof of my cart?"

"Sorry. I'm Alek. I was Kindra's guard back in Dredfall and—"

"You're the kid? Kindra was pretty upset that she didn't get to say goodbye to you! She's going to be thrilled when she finds out she didn't miss her chance."

Alek tried to get to the point. "Listen, I know they are all out there having a grand time decapitating giants and turning creatures to mist, but you need to get this cart moving."

"Alek, you seem very sweet and I'm sure you mean well, but if I leave this lot here in the woods, they will never speak to me again."

"Just get the wagon moving! They can jump aboard if they don't want to be left behind. I've seen the monsters Skilanis keeps as pets. If he has sent the creatures your friends are currently battling, worse creatures are soon to arrive."

Alek was becoming more anxious by the second. He needed to get the driver to understand the danger of sitting still.

"The hundespor hunt this forest. I am sure they have heard all this commotion. If they decide to pursue us, they will easily overtake this wagon. We need to be gone before they join this attack!"

Frida seemed to be ready to continue the argument when the door to the wagon swung open. Trego leaned out of the cart and looked up at Alek. His eyes glowed silver in the dark. Alek was enthralled for a second. The male was speaking to him, but Alek did not understand. Alek shook his head to clear it.

"You worked in the kennels, boy?"

Alek just nodded. He was still staring at the male's eyes.

"You say these are Skilanis's creatures?"

Alek nodded again.

Trego turned to yell to Frida. "The boy knows things we do not. Get this wagon moving and yell to the others to load up. Kindra can hold them back as we make a run for it."

As Frida snapped the reins and called to Kindra to hold off the horde, Trego beckoned Alek inside the wagon. Alek lifted himself from the roof and floated himself gently to the entrance and into the wagon. He turned to pull the door closed behind him, but Trego placed a hand on his wrist.

"Leave it open for the others," Trego instructed.

Trego opened the door on the opposite side of the cart as well. The wagon was gaining speed, and the resistance created was pinning the doors open helpfully. Joral and Leif appeared inside the wagon in a blink. Capable of teleportation, both males had simply needed to envision themselves within the confines of the cart, and then give themselves a little push. Gunnar could not teleport, but had been relatively close to the left side of the wagon when Frida had called out that she was on the move. He had run for a few yards and then grabbed hold of the cart and swung himself through the door. Bane could be seen through the open door. He made the leap for the box up front where Frida was loudly urging the horses to run. Krish and Kindra remained outside of the wagon. Leif started laughing.

"What do you find so amusing, brother?" asked Gunnar. "Your daughter is out there and in grave danger."

"My daughter is able to teleport. She can actually make the jump farther than any of us in this wagon can. She'll be fine. I'm laughing because that arrogant prince she wants to marry is going to have to wait for Kindra to rescue him from those monsters because he can't teleport. The heir to the throne, the same person who lightheartedly looks down his nose at us all, is at the mercy of my half-human daughter. I think the thought of her blinking them both into the wagon right before our eyes is good cause for a chuckle."

Gunnar rolled his eyes. He should have known Leif would find it amusing that Krish was weak in magical ability. Gunnar, also weak in magic when compared to his traveling companions, did not find anything about the current situation funny. Kindra appeared on the bench beside Gunnar, pulling him from his thoughts. Krish crashed to the floor at the feet of those already in the cart. Kindra lunged for him to be sure he was not injured.

"I am so sorry, Krish. I swear! I pictured you landing right next to Trego! I didn't expect there to be someone—"

Kindra stopped talking and turned her head to look at the person occupying the place on the bench next to the healer. Her eyes went wide, and then a huge smile dawned, lighting up her entire face. She threw herself at Alek and wrapped her arms around him. Krish, still on the floor, cleared his throat.

"As I was saying," said Krish. "I'm fine. There is no need to worry about me. By all means, go hug the little urchin and leave me here on the floor."

"Krish!" Kindra spun to face her future husband. "I'm so sorry. It's just that this is the boy I was telling you about. This is my friend Alek. He took care of me while I was locked in the kennels."

"Took care of you?" Leif laughed. "He introduced himself to me as your guard."

"That too, I suppose," replied Kindra. "He did get me food, water, and all the books I wanted."

Gunnar gave Alek a wink. "Sorry, lad. Sounds like you had your work cut out for you."

The wagon hit something on the path that bounced all the occupants into the air. Gunnar, one of the tallest of the group, hit his head on the roof.

"You deserved that," said Kindra.

"If Bane hadn't joined Frida up front, he would have shared in my pain. Would that have been fair?" asked Gunnar, rubbing his head.

"If you are referring to Bane being taller than you are, I am of similar height and was spared hitting my head, as I am bent down tending to our Crown Prince," said Trego.

Alek, picking up on the injustice perceived by Krish and Trego, vacated his seat and placed his bottom on the floor of the wagon. Krish made his way to the wooden bench and sat down.

"Thank you, lad. I feared I might remain on that floor forever with this lot arguing around me," Krish said to Alek.

Alek gave Krish a small nod. Joral banged on the wall at the front of the wagon.

"Frida, how are you faring out there?" yelled Joral.

Frida's voice was breathy, but loud when she replied, "All good up here. I don't think we are being pursued."

"Slow us down a tad, then?" asked Joral. "There is no need to toss a wheel or break an axle. We can move swiftly without wearing out the horses."

Frida did not reply, but the speed of the wagon's movement decreased noticeably. No longer needing to yell to hear one another, everyone looked to the floor of the wagon for an explanation. Kindra sat at Krish's feet, once again hugging the small Elven boy who had been Kindra's guard when she'd seen him last, and seemingly appeared in the wagon by magic moments ago. It was Leif who spoke first.

"We can probably stop and let the kid out now. I'm sure he didn't intend to stray this far from Fallholm."

Kindra stared daggers at Leif. "It does not matter if he intended to be this far from that cesspool; he gets to stay with us. If we let Alek go in the forest, the hundespor will make a meal of him. If Alek makes it back through the Dredskog, Skilanis will have him killed because I escaped under his watch."

Alek was having trouble breathing with his face mushed against Kindra. Her affection genuinely surprised and touched him, and he was happy to know she considered him a friend, but the protective embrace was excessive. He wiggled free by ducking his head under one of her arms and looked around at the group of people staring back from the benches lining the walls.

"I um... I really don't have anywhere to go," Alek admitted. "I figured the Master would have me killed once he saw Kindra was gone, so I jumped on top of the wagon when Bane and Trego smuggled her out of the kennel. I um... I didn't think about what happens next."

"What about the family you left behind?" asked Joral. "Won't they be wondering what happened to you?"

Alek replied solemnly, "I have no family in Dredfall."

"Do you have any family outside of this kingdom?" asked Joral. "Once we arrive in Lillerem, we could help you find them."

"I actually don't know," Alek said sadly. "I assumed I was born as a slave, but I must have some family somewhere."

At this, Kindra perked up. "That would be my department. I am exceptional at finding lost family. I should warn you though; sometimes what I find is not exactly what people were looking for."

Kindra gave Leif a hard stare. It had been less than a year ago that Kindra's own hunt for missing family members had led her to discover Leif was her father. That had then led Kindra to discover Alfheim, and then to discover she was an Elven Princess. Well, half-Elven Princess. Kindra's mother, killed by Ulford's Elite Guard, had been human.

Leif cocked his head. "Well then, if we're stuck with you anyway, tell us about Skilanis's monsters, Alek."

CHAPTER 5

Skilanis reached down into the puddle of skin, blood, and bone fragments to pick up the golden ring of thorns. He placed Ulford's crown of twisted vines on his own head. The living soldiers on the parade ground dropped to one knee and placed their right arms across their chests. The dead soldiers enlarged the gore puddle in the sand.

Captain Johan Bakken looked up at Skilanis as the new king surveyed the carnage before him. Bakken's choice to support Skilanis was fueled by years of perceived injustice at the hands of Ulford. Now Captain of the Second Draw, Bakken should have held the position many decades ago. He had been on the front line when Ulford carved out a swath of the Kingdom of Lillerem and made it his own. Bakken had personally dispatched the majority of Ulford's strongest opponents, Ulford's own family, on the day the Kingdom of Dredfall was created. Ulford's sister Ekkelle, and all of her descendants had been the only obstacles preventing Ulford from declaring himself king of the new territory. At Ekkelles's home, Bakken had killed every living soul while the rest of the army stormed Castle Bindrell.

That act should have ensured Bakken's promotion. However, a young soldier named Syndral had ambushed Ekkelle on her way to aid her family in their last stand at the farmstead. Syndral had been the soldier to kill Ulford's sister, and so Syndral had been promoted to captain of the Second Draw.

After years of serving under the female who had stolen his promotion, Bakken finally earned the rank of captain. At the Battle of Millspare, Lieutenant Johan Bakken had met Syndral's stare as she fell from her mount with an arrow protruding from her side. The look she gave him told Bakken she was silently passing command of the Second Draw to him. Bakken had taken the Second Draw straight to the gates of the castle. From just behind his line of soldiers, he sensed that the gate was about to fall. That was when his entire draw had frozen like statues. Bakken and his horse were fixed in place. Fire started to rain down from the castle walls at the tips of arrows. Bakken could do nothing but watch his men burn and listen to them scream.

Johan had learned later that Kindra, the female half-elf princess from the human realm, had been the one to freeze the soldiers where they stood around the castle. Her magic had sentenced thousands of soldiers to death. When flames approached Bakken's horse, the creature had pulled from Kindra's mental grasp and fled. Bakken was carried to safety by the steed. Only a score of soldiers from the Second Draw had survived that battle. Of those, Ulford had officially promoted Bakken to captain.

Now, staring up at his new king, Captain Bakken was well aware that it had been this man who had shown him appreciation. Skilanis, a member of the First Draw, hadn't felt respected by Ulford either. When the First Draw was ordered to the human realm to hunt down and kill human descendants of the last great king of Lillerem, Skilanis had participated minimally. Instead of perpetrating attacks himself, he had requested that the members of the First Draw remove select bones from the victims in the human realm. In exchange for the bones, Skilanis lent the services of his hundespor to locate Elven blood by smell. The result was that targets were identified in the human realm with speed and efficiency. The hundespor were restricted from making the kills so that bones from the dead could be saved for Skilanis. Death by hundespor did not always leave bones behind.

Skilanis motioned for Bakken to rise. Johan climbed to his feet and took a position at the right side of the new king.

"I'm sorry your plan did not unfold as expected," Bakken said to Skilanis.

"I was disappointed that the princes could not dispatch Ulford as part of their rescue mission. It would've prevented the need for all this."

Skilanis swept his hand to indicate the growing puddle of putrescence.

"Our primary objective is complete," Skilanis continued. "I have taken the Dredfall throne. Unfortunately, I had to use my favorite pets for the task. Imra can't feel their intentions the way she would have felt mine if I had committed the deed myself. Having so many of my babies here provides Kindra and the princes a better chance of making it back to Lillerem."

"Regarding Imra," Bakken began, "we have yet to find her."

"I am unconcerned," Skilanis replied. "Imra is no warrior and she no longer has her beloved Ulford to manipulate. She is little threat to me. Once we call our first World Destroyer from Muspelheim, Imra and the pests from Lillerem will be inconsequential."

Johan did not know much about how Skilanis pulled beings into Alfheim from other worlds. He was aware that none of the new king's pets originated in this realm. He also knew none of the otherworldly creatures previously brought to Alfheim were from Muspelheim, the realm of fire. Skilanis had a collection of very specific bones from humans with Elven blood. Somehow, Skilanis planned to use them to obtain powerful creatures, capable of destroying entire worlds, from the realm of fire. Captain Bakken had tentative faith in Skilanis's ability to control the new creatures in the same way he commanded his current gruesome menagerie.

"It's time for our next task, Bakken. I need the five separate bones of a skull."

Bakken looked around the training yard and saw several skulls. He took a few steps toward one lying on the ground to his right.

"It can't be just any skull," said Skilanis. "The five bones must not have fused yet. The skull must come from a child."

Bakken's stomach lurched. He was willing to do anything required of him to support Skilanis, but he did not want to kill a child. Bakken had been raised in the children's barracks of the slave quarters. He still visited the barracks often to bring toys and clothes to the young slaves. Having the trust of the children would make it easy to kill one for its five skull bones, but it also made him nauseous to think about betraying that trust.

Skilanis continued, "The five unfused bones must come from a powerful Elven child. After Ulford eradicated all challengers to the throne in this realm, there were no children with powerful magic here in Alfheim. I expanded my search. My hundespor were stalking an Elven child in the human realm, but she seems to have vanished. It can only mean she left that realm and is hiding here. Begin your search by listening for rumors of children wielding magic. It does not need to be a grand expression of power. The child may be hiding the full strength of magic they control."

Imra pushed through the brush that ran along the river outside of Fallholm. Twigs and pricker bushes tore at her gown as she tried to walk along the muddy riverbank in her heeled sandals. She was not dressed for this forced excursion. Imra had hoped the seductive dress would prove to be a fun way to keep the princes distracted while her lover ensconced himself among his soldiers on the parade grounds. Leaving the castle had not been part of Imra's evening plans. She needed to find a place where she could sit down and think for a moment.

Detaining the princes had been entertaining at first. They used almost no magic to dispatch twenty-five trained men. The show ceased being pleasurable the moment she could no longer draw breath. At least one of the princes in that throne room had possessed incredible power. Imra had not felt anything to predict the magic was about to be used. As soon as her throat was released, she had fled.

Imra had gone straight to the parade grounds to join Ulford, where she could also be protected by his soldiers. She had been surprised, for the second time this evening, upon her arrival. She watched from the stairway above the grounds as Skilanis picked up Ulford's crown from a floor covered in blood, and positioned it on his head. The male did not even wipe it clean before doing so. Soldiers kneeled and crossed their chests, Skilanis's repulsive beasts prowled the perimeter, and Imra ran. She did not stop running as she left the castle grounds and entered the streets of Fallholm. She passed through the city gates where the male on watch was not aware of the treason she had left behind her. Waving the guard off when he asked if she needed assistance, she made her way along the outside of the city wall to the river, where she was now struggling through the mud.

Imra knew she had covered several miles when she reached the neighboring village at last. There was a jetty protruding into the water and Imra walked out to the end of it and crumpled to a seated position on the wooden boards. She hung her bare feet over the water. Her sandals had not lasted long in the mud. Imra's eyes had remained dry as she single-mindedly put distance between herself and Castle Bindrell, but now, the tears started. With her body at rest, and no immediate goal, her mind was awash with all she had witnessed and the ramifications of those events.

"Believe me, honey, he ain't worth waterworks," said a voice from behind Imra.

She twisted her head to look over her shoulder. A once-beautiful female with dark skin stood a few feet behind Imra on the dock. A jagged scar marred the otherwise perfect complexion of her face. The scar ran from the center of her temple down through her right eye socket. That socket was an empty hole. Imra was not going to disclose all of her secrets to the stranger, but she felt the need to talk to someone.

"I just don't know what I'm going to do without him," said Imra.

The female smiled knowingly. "Child, we all feel lost when we lose something we have known as part of us. The thing you need to remember is that he only felt as if he was a piece of your whole. You are still you. You have lost nothing of yourself."

"We were together for so many years. I have nowhere to go. I don't remember who I am without him." Imra sobbed quietly.

"You will," said the female. "My name is Tomia. Come. Let's get you cleaned up and see if we can start rediscovering the female you think you've lost."

Imra climbed to her feet and followed Tomia to a metal shack just yards away. From the outside, Imra couldn't imagine the building provided enough space for two people. There was a crooked chimney pipe protruding from the corrugated roof, and tendrils of smoke spiraled from it. The door creaked loudly when Tomia pulled it open, and a blast of warm air rushed to greet Imra. As uncertain as she felt about entering the shanty, Imra craved the warmth and followed Tomia inside.

A small wood-burning stove stood in the far right corner of the single room. Giving the place a cursory look, Imra decided the stove was the highest-valued item Tomia possessed. There was a sleeping pallet, raised about six inches from the floor and covered in a patchwork quilt. There was also a wooden crate, and a set of free-standing shelves that were piled with everything from books to cutlery. It seemed every item Tomia owned was displayed on those shelves.

Tomia turned the crate over and sat on it, then motioned for Imra to take a seat on the make-shift bed. Imra sat down hard. She had been expecting some kind of mattress, but now suspected the pallet had been created by covering wooden crates, such as the one Tomia was using as a chair. Tomia smiled at Imra's fleeting discomfort.

"I expect you are accustomed to something slightly more luxurious," said Tomia.

Imra was embarrassed. She fumbled for the right words to explain that she wasn't judging the woman, but had only been momentarily surprised that the bed was so hard. She gave up and simply lowered her head to stare at the floor.

"There are no worries, child," said Tomia. "It wasn't your reaction to my home or my bed that gave you away. I fear you have forgotten about the dress you are wearing. I don't suppose it's much of a dress anymore, but it looks as if it was once beautiful."

Tomia bent at the waist from her seated position on the crate and lifted the quilt next to Imra's legs. Tomia pulled out a drawer, created by inserting one crate into another. It was an ingenious and practical use of the wooden boxes. From the drawer, Tomia withdrew a plain wool dress. When Imra realized the female meant to offer the frock to her, she immediately shook her head.

"I can't take your clothes!" ...*Especially when you obviously own so little and I'm really not sure if that dress is crawling with fleas or mites. Please, just accept my...*

Tomia interrupted Imra's frantic thoughts. "I assure you, though not fancy, the dress is clean. Besides, you will leave me your dress in exchange."

Imra was beginning to suspect that Tomia might be able to read her mind. She was not sure if this was a true magical gift, or if Tomia was simply good at reading people, but Imra decided to be careful with her thoughts. Imra nodded and Tomia placed the clean, well-worn dress beside her, atop of the quilt.

"I'll go draw some fresh water so you can clean up a bit," said Tomia.

The female opened the creaking metal door and disappeared. Imra took the time alone to inspect the wool dress Tomia had provided. There were no holes and there appeared to be no bugs crawling among the fibers.

Tomia returned with a bucket of water and a cloth. She handed both to Imra and Imra scooped the cool water onto her face to wash away some of the grime, then used the cloth on her arms and legs. She started scrubbing the mud and blood from her ankles and bare feet.

"I have no shoes to offer, but it is of no concern. Most here don't wear them. You would not blend well with the villagers if you were to have a pair and claim to be a person of no consequence," said Tomia.

Imra stripped off her torn and damp gown and let it fall into a pile on the dirt floor. She pulled the wool dress on and smoothed it down over her body. It was warm, though it did nothing for Imra's figure, and the material was scratchy.

"Stay the night here. When you have rested, you can then begin your journey of rediscovery."

Imra wanted to argue with the older female, but she had no energy left. Without another word, Imra gave in to overwhelming exhaustion and lay back on the bed. She was asleep before she even thought to thank Tomia for her kindness.

CHAPTER 6

Captain Bakken stepped from the children's barracks of the slave quarters. He had found over fifty slave children living at the barracks, but none with any magical ability. One of the younger boys had provided information that might prove to have made his visit worthwhile, though. The young elf spoke of a boy named Alek who played football with the kids from the barracks, and the boy had magical ability. Alek denied his ability to the other children, but the children had seen the football do unnatural things in his presence.

Bakken had checked in with the caretaker at the barracks in an attempt to locate the boy. The grumpy male did little more than keep a record of which bunk was assigned to which child, and then notify Skilanis when a slave child came of age for the move to the adult slave quarters. The caretaker had shared that Alek had not been to the barracks in several weeks. He informed Bakken that Alek was on special assignment at the kennels, and Captain Bakken sets out to find the boy.

With luck, Alek would be powerful enough for Skilanis to use him as the source for his five unfused skull bones. Once Bakken procured those bones for Dredfall's new king, Skilanis would call this world destroying beast to this realm and easily become the ruler of all of Alfheim. It sounded easy as Bakken reviewed the plan in his head. The part that made Bakken nervous was that the ability to call a World Ender from Muspelheim relied on the use of these skull bones and he was the one tasked with getting them. Playing such a pivotal role in Skilanis's grand plan was an honor, but would result in catastrophe for Bakken if he failed in his task.

Captain Bakken felt unease as he approached the entrance to the kennels. It was not Kindra's absence causing that disquiet. He knew Skilanis was aware of Kindra's escape. It was the one part of Skilanis's plan that had flowed flawlessly. Kindra was held as bait for the princes. The princes achieved their primary goal and rescued Kindra, but Imra had foreseen Ulford's fate and prevented the princes from encountering him during the attack.

The incessant barking that usually emanated from the kennels was disturbingly absent. Bakken walked through the passages and found no one. Tobias, the houndsman, was gone, and so were the hounds. The doors to the dogs' cages stood open as if they had been set free. The cages for Skilanis's pets were empty. Most of the beasts were tracking down Kindra and the princes in the Dredskog. The hundespor, having finished up at the parade grounds, would have joined the other beasts on the hunt by now. Kindra's cage was empty as expected, but Bakken's concern was that Alek was not to be found anywhere in these kennels.

Bakken leaned against the unyielding stone wall and was pensive. He suspected Tobias and Alek had fled to avoid Skilanis's wrath. Though Tobias was not technically responsible for Kindra, the houndsman would expect to be punished for her escape. Bakken speculated about Alek's absence. Tobias had likely freed the dogs. The old male had probably convinced Alek to leave to avoid punishment for losing the princess. It was possible they left together to take their chances running through the forest to Lillerem. Others had done the same, but few made it out of the Dredskog safely. Unfortunately for Bakken, he needed to ensure Alek's head stayed in one piece; at least until the time came for Dredfall's new king to split it.

With only his own suspicions to work with, Bakken left the kennels to ask around in the market. Kindra was liberated from the kennels after dusk. Most of the merchants would have already closed up shop, but they would have still been in the market square balancing books for the day's sales. Unfortunately for Bakken, it was now approaching the middle of the night and there were very few people in the streets, let alone a marketplace full of witnesses. Postponing the search for Alek until morning was not an option.

Captain Bakken crossed the square to the apothecary. The shop window displayed advertisements boasting of the miracle cures inside. Next to the shop entrance was a door leading to the apartment above. Bakken pushed the door to enter, but it was locked. Bakken knocked and then waited. He banged a little louder, and was rewarded with the sound of feet stomping down a flight of stairs.

There was a sound of a deadbolt being pulled back and the door swung open to reveal a very perturbed looking old elf. The look on the merchant's face would have silenced many soldiers, but Bakken was struck by what the elf was wearing on his head.

"Sir! Are you really wearing a sleeping cap?" Bakken blurted.

"It's the middle of the night. What else would I have on my head?"

"I just thought sleeping caps were so long out of fashion, I imagined I would never see one," Bakken answered.

"Piss off!"

The shopkeeper started closing the door, but Bakken stuck his foot between it and the door jamb. With the shock of seeing a person wearing an actual night cap fading, Bakken realized he was being foolish and very unprofessional. He was here for information, and insulting the old merchant was not going to win him any favor.

"Sir," Bakken tried again. "Forgive me. The article of clothing reminded me of my dear father and it sent a shock to my system. I meant no harm, nor insult by my foolish comments. I am sorry to have disturbed you, but the Crown seeks to find a runaway slave and I'm hoping you may have information that may prove to be helpful."

The merchant softened, but only slightly. When a slave ran from Dredfall, things were tense for everyone until the escapee was found. The soldiers were not permitted to rest until the slave was recovered alive or sufficient time had passed to assume the runaway had fallen to the creatures of the Dredskog.

"If you're talking about tonight, I saw the hounds run," said the merchant. "I was already in the shop, restocking my shelves, but it was impossible to miss the sound of their baying as they sprang from the kennel. I watched through the window as they all ran in separate directions."

"Was the houndsman with them?" asked Bakken asked.

"Tobias? Yeah, he came limping out with the last of them. I don't know where he went, though. It was already dark and it ain't like he was baying like the hounds were."

"Did you see which way the apprentice went?"

"I never saw the boy. You never know with that one, though. I don't trust him. He's always sneakin' round the marketplace. Ya gotta watch him close."

"Thank you, sir. Sorry to have woken you. You have been helpful."

"Night now," said the merchant as he shut his door.

With proof Tobias had left of his own accord, Bakken decided his theory that the houndsman and his apprentice had fled for Lillerem together was the most likely scenario. There were no longer any hounds to track the runaways, and Skilanis's pets would be occupied with the hunt for Kindra and the princes. Though it made finding Tobias and Alek more difficult, Bakken hoped that would improve the chances of finding Tobias and Alek whole, or even alive.

Bakken went to the stables to ready his horse. He sent a runner to summon the Second Draw, and the soldiers started to arrive minutes later. Some were still rubbing sleep from their eyes, and others were chewing licorice in an attempt to hide the drink they had lately been enjoying. All managed to be ready to thunder from the stalls in thirty minutes.

"Men, we have no hounds on this expedition. I can only assume the dogs have taken to the streets or joined our quarry in their escape. We are tracking the houndsman, Tobias, and his apprentice. The apprentice is called Alek, and he is a young elf of about forty summers," Bakken explained to his men.

"Sir?" a lieutenant called for Bakken's attention. "We're hunting a child and an elderly male?"

"It's the child we are hunting, but they left the kennels together," replied Bakken. "Any other questions?"

The soldiers met the question with silence.

"Ok, then," Bakken said. "The boy is of particular interest to our new king. Take the boy alive. Do what you will with the kennelmaster."

A few looks were exchanged between the soldiers, but no one spoke. Bakken nodded, and the soldiers rode from the stables headed for the Dredskog.

Unaware of the outcome of the rescue mission carried out earlier in the evening, Syndral paced the living room floor of Leif's cabin in the human realm. Her plan had been to sleep at the cabin this evening, and then make the trip through the portal to Aergroth so she could arrive at Millspare in time for breakfast tomorrow. Her plans had derailed. When Syndral arrived at the cabin, Jess and her German Shepherd dogs, Butch and Cassidy, were already at the cabin. Jess, too, planned to make an early start through the portal and thought sleeping at the cabin would facilitate the early morning journey. Secretly, Syndral wondered if Jess was also looking for a little time away from her husband, Sean. By all accounts, things between Jess and Sean seemed to be going well, but Syndral understood the part of Jess that was fiercely independent. Syndral was willing to gamble Jess was looking forward to a few nights away from her husband. The couple had only recently started to resolve some of the distance that had come between them while Jess had been journeying between Alfheim and the human realm over the last few months.

Jess and her dogs were currently sacked out in Leif's giant bed, behind a locked door. Even if Syndral had been first to claim the bed, she still would not be sleeping. Nerves had driven Syndral to throw her blankets off and rise from the couch. She felt this way every time she prepared to see her daughter, and pacing seemed to be the only way to burn off some of the anxiety. When Syndral introduced herself to Riva several weeks ago, the little girl had immediately known Syndral was her mother. It was the most wonderful feeling Syndral had ever experienced.

That feeling had faded quickly and been replaced with the gnawing sensation that no matter what she did, Syndral was doing everything wrong. Syndral had given her daughter up to a human couple shortly after Riva was born, so Riva could be raised safely in the human realm. It had worked well, but as a result, Syndral hadn't been a part of her own daughter's life for forty years. Riva was now in her adolescence, and Syndral was, only now, learning to be a mother.

Syndral and Riva reunited a short time ago, after the girl's life had been threatened by Ulford's assassins and the hundespor had started to hunt her. Jess was instrumental in that reunion and Syndral had been hopeful that it would be the beginning of a new life. The new life was delayed by the need to shuffle Riva off to Millspare as a means to protect the girl. Syndral had then needed to keep her distance so she would not lead Ulford and his army to Riva's location.

On her first visit to Millspare to see Riva after Ulford's assassins were driven from the human realm, Syndral had brought Riva a stuffed dog. For most girls Riva's age, this would have been a childish gift, but Riva always kept a stuffed animal in her backpack to pet when she was scared, so Syndral had felt the gift was perfect. When Riva saw the adorable stuffed Labrador, her reaction had not been disdain for the plush toy, but absolute outrage that Syndral would bring a fake dog instead of a real one. Syndral, foolishly expecting her daughter to take the stuffed toy and cuddle with it gratefully, had not reacted well to Riva's outburst. Between expletives, Syndral had called Riva unappreciative and had turned on her heel and left Millspare.

The next visit had been only slightly better. On that occasion, Syndral was eating lunch in the kitchen with the kindly cook, Einar, when Riva came down to join them. Riva told Syndral about her tutors and the things she was learning with them and Syndral managed to nod along and look interested. When Riva paused to take a bite of her sandwich, Syndral asked if Riva had met any of the children from the town of Aergroth. Riva burst into tears and ran from the room.

Einar quickly explained to Syndral that Mildred, who acted as a nanny of sorts to Riva, had proclaimed just that morning that Riva was not to venture into Aergroth on her own. One of the arguments Riva had made for wanting to take the trip was to make some friends. It was still a very raw wound when Syndral brought it up.

Syndral was extremely thankful to Einar and Mildred for looking after Riva. The older Elven couple had helped raise all the princes, in one way or another, and were more than happy to extend their love to Riva. Einar and Mildred were not the issue. The problem was Syndral, and she knew it.

As Syndral paced the floor, she tried to make up her mind. On one hand, living at Millspare and raising her daughter with Einar and Mildred there to help seemed like the path of least resistance. Just when Syndral felt ready to commit to that choice, memories of attacking that same castle as the commander of Ulford's Second Draw would flood her mind. She would remember why she had previously declined the offer to stay at Millspare.

Another option was to bring Riva back to the human realm and continue to raise her here. It would require moving around every few years to hide the fact that Riva aged so slowly, but Leif and Gunnar were evidence that it could be accomplished. Both princes had been sent to the human realm by their mother when they were children. They were raised by a kind family in Norway and kept safely out of King Ulford's reach. Thoughts of Leif invaded Syndral's mind. He was an elf who had overstayed his welcome in the human realm by about a hundred years, and now he really didn't belong anywhere. He was incapable of moving through a society of humans successfully, but he knew very little about his Elven roots and family. Syndral did not want that for Riva.

Syndral sat down hard on the couch. She was being ridiculous. As Riva's mother, the only thing she needed to consider was what was best for Riva. Riva should be raised among elves in Alfheim. Syndral curled up and threw her blanket over herself. In the morning, she would travel through the portal and see her daughter. If all went as planned, she would also be seeing Kindra for the first time since the woman had been abducted from the human realm. At least that would distract Syndral's mind from the pressure to be the perfect mother.

CHAPTER 7

The merchant wagon emerged from the Dredskog and into Lillerem at the Kingdom's northern-most point. Frida and Bane had taken turns driving the horses through the night. They had started at a run, slowed to a trot and eventually settled on a walk, but decided it was better not to stop completely. At this point, the horses were not the only ones who needed to rest. There was no reason Skilanis's creatures couldn't follow the group into Lillerem, but it was unlikely they would do so with the sun rising. The hundespor were comfortable in the bright sun of the open countryside, but there was no cover for the beasts here and the group would see them emerge from the forest.

Bane stopped at a stream in order for the horses to drink. The wagon's passengers unloaded from the cramped quarters to stretch and regain circulation in their extremities. Alek turned in a full circle once he stepped away from the wagon. He turned a second time before Trego stepped up beside him. The flamboyantly-dressed healer placed his hand on Alek's shoulder.

"I remember my first day in Lillerem. I couldn't believe how green everything was. I felt like the fields went on forever."

"Do the people live underground?" asked Alek.

Trego chuckled. "No. They live in houses and castles the same as they do in most places. The difference in Lillerem is the space. Those in Lillerem have the luxury of spreading out and living anywhere in the Kingdom. In the lands we come from, there are few places worth making a life, so everyone does it in the same area."

"Where are you from?" Alek asked Trego.

"Originally? I was born in the Kingdom of Kanoma, on the other side of the salt lake. My family left there for a chance at a better life before I saw fifteen summers. We lived in the Kingdom of Aldair, just south of Lillerem, for a time."

Trego had gained an audience. Kindra and Gunnar were also listening to the healer's story. Though Trego's accent hinted that he was not originally from Lillerem, Kindra had felt it would be rude to ask too many questions. That was a definite advantage to having a child around. He could ask all the uncomfortable questions, and had no idea that others might consider it impolite.

"Why didn't you stay in Aldair?" asked Alek.

"When I was a little older than you, Aldair's king outlawed magic, but it was safe to conceal magical abilities simply by refraining from using them. The king didn't actively hunt magic wielders. Alas, I come from a family of healers. My parents found it impossible to stand by and watch people suffer when they knew they could be of service. One day they used magic to save someone's life, and the king heard of the act. My parents were hanged in the middle of the capital city and left as carrion for the birds; a reminder to the citizens that magic was forbidden," said Trego solemnly.

Krish picked up the story. "I was unaware of all that occurred before you entered Lillerem. The rest of the story is recorded in the archives for all to read, and Trego's modesty always prevents him from telling the whole tale. My grandfather, Lars, was hunting large game in the bushlands bordering Aldair. Lars managed to corner a boar and was poised to make the kill. When he turned in his saddle to spear the boar, the horse was spooked and Lars was thrown from the horse's back. The horse took off at a run and the boar gored Lars in the face and stomach. Both wounds were excruciating, but neither caused immediate death. Lars was alive, but would never have lived long enough to make it back to the palace to see the healers.

"The young Trego watched the attack from the brush. The stories say he was just walking along, but I suspect he was hungry and hoping to ask for the opportunity to share some boar around the hunters' fire. Regardless, Trego could not leave someone holding his own guts in his hands. He healed the hunter, only discovering later that the male he had saved was the Crown Prince of Lillerem. His deed earned Trego a permanent place at Gulentine Palace."

Alek's mouth hung open. "You saved the future king of Lillerem and you didn't even know it! That's badass!"

Trego, not accustomed to the open awe of a child, reddened and tried to hide his smile. Bane saved the healer from further praise. The giant male let out a loud whistle to indicate it was time to get back in the wagon. Alek looked as if he might start peppering Trego with more questions, but caught the stern look Kindra sent his way. Alek shrugged, unsure why he was getting the look, but understanding the meaning behind it.

Gunnar joined Frida on the driver's box and the others entered the wagon to find Bane's presence making the quarters even more cramped. It would take several hours to get to Smalgroth. There, Frida would part ways with the group and return to her home. The others would retrieve their horses from the stable and continue on to Castle Millspare in Aergroth.

Imra rolled over and opened her eyes. Her body ached everywhere. The events of the previous night flooded back, and understanding dawned. Trudging through mud in an evening gown and heels the night before, explained the soreness in her muscles. The exertion had been equivalent to Imra's usual exercise for an entire week. Sleeping on a bed of wooden crates had not lessened the discomfort she now felt.

Imra sat up and looked around the shack. It looked different from how she remembered it from the previous night. The extra crate where Tomia sat was still in the center of the floor, but the shelves standing against the corrugated metal wall were empty. By the time Imra arrived at Tomia's little shack the night before, she was exhausted. It was possible she had imagined the shelves to be as she remembered them simply because it made sense for them to be piled with detritus. Tomia seemed like the type to hoard things she might need at some point, even if they seemed useless at the moment.

Rubbing her eyes, Imra leaned over and pulled the bucket of water Tomia had brought for her last night a little closer. The rag was still inside and Imra ran it over her face and neck to help pull herself further from sleep. The metal shack was quickly being heated by the sun, and Imra needed to get out into the air. She grabbed the bucket, intending to use the water to douse the coals in the stove before she left. Saving the shack from an unattended fire proved to be an unnecessary task. There was no stove.

Imra distinctly remembered thinking the stove had been the most expensive item Tomia had in her shack. Either Imra had been in worse shape last night than she thought, or something about the shack was not as it should be. Imra stood and discovered an advantage to the plain dress provided by Tomia. The material did not wrinkle. Imra smoothed it down quickly anyway, more out of habit, and then swung the noisy metal door open to greet the day.

Once outside of the shack, Imra recalled her lack of shoes. She carefully picked her way barefoot over rocks and tree roots as she moved farther from the river and toward the village Tomia had suggested was nearby. Imra climbed a grassy hill and savored the feel of the softer earth on the raw skin of her feet for a moment. She could hear the sounds of civilization now and adjusted her course slightly to meet it.

After trekking a short distance through a wooded area and sustaining additional cuts on her feet, Imra stood at the edge of a dirt road. A horse and wagon waited to her left and was shortly boarded by a farmer in a plain dress not unlike the one Imra was wearing. Imra was surprised to see the elf was barefoot. Unlike Imra, the farmer did not appear to notice pebbles or other obstacles on the ground. This was only more evidence to speed Imra's realization that her comfortable lifestyle had left her under-prepared for her current situation.

The inn on the other side of the road beckoned Imra, as her stomach called for food. Unfortunately, Tomia had not filled the pockets of the dress before offering it to Imra, and Imra had no coin of her own. Sighing, Imra approached the farmer atop the wagon instead.

"Pardon me," said Imra. "I'm trying to get my bearings. I need to cross through the Dredskog and into Lillerem."

The farmer was so shocked, she did not reply right away. Imra did not even notice. Three Dredfall soldiers had emerged from the inn across the street. Imra held her breath as she waited for them to notice her. She prepared herself to be dragged back to Castle

Bindrell, making her desperate escape of last night pointless. She would be dead before luncheon. Instead of crossing the street to collect Imra, the soldiers mounted horses and thundered off down the road.

"Ah," said the farmer, watching Imra observe the soldiers' departure. "I suppose telling you to just keep following this road won't work?"

"Uh… no," Imra replied hesitantly. "I should prefer to stay off the roads if it is possible."

The farmer thought for a moment and then asked, "How's your sense of direction?"

"Good," Imra replied, relieved that it was the truth.

"In that case, you do have the option to take a much shorter route," said the farmer. "If you go directly south from this village, ignoring all roads and paths, it is the shortest distance to Lillerem you will find."

"Thank you," replied Imra. "I'm all for taking the fastest route."

The farmer smiled. "I never said it was the fastest route, and I didn't say it would be easy either. All I said was that it was the shortest route and it will keep you off the roads. Good luck to ya."

The farmer made a clicking noise with her tongue and her cart rolled off. Imra looked beyond the inn and into the forest. All she had to do was walk a straight line until she emerged from the woods. Imra laughed quietly. Expeditions such as the one before her had been one of the things that caused Imra to be more of a strategist than a fighter. Though she had technically been a member of the First Draw, Imra knew she was no soldier. Imra preferred to leave the dirt, camps, weapons, blood and fighting to others. Her battlefield was in her mind.

She crossed the street and made her way along the side of the inn. The smell of bacon nearly drove her mad as she passed by an open window. Behind the building, Imra reached the edge of the forest and took several steps into the cover of the trees. She stood there for a moment, taking in the sounds of the birds and the rustle of small animals in the leaves. It was just another forest. All she needed to do was find a place on the horizon to set her gaze so she could walk straight into Lillerem.

Imra didn't move. This forest was dense. It was impossible to see more than a few hundred yards ahead, let alone to the horizon. The moment she walked around a tree or boulder, she would be slightly off-course. Imra was too smart to think this was going to be easy. *Use your strengths, Imra. You're intelligent. Think this through. What was it they said about moss? Did it grow on the north side of trees?*

Imra closed her eyes. She let her magic swirl within her body. She felt it warming her blood and surrounding her. Imra took a deep breath and released it slowly. She needed to be calm and trust that her gift would carry her where she needed to go. Imra opened her eyes and took a few steps. She walked around the trunk of a giant tree and felt a slight tug at her body as her magic corrected her course. As the farmer suggested, this would not be the fastest route, but Imra's brand of magic would ensure it was the safest route.

Imra continued through the woods with no major incidents for over an hour. She wished she had asked the farmer how long the journey would take. Her magic would guide her on the safest route and Imra was willing to turn navigation over to that power, but she was finding it difficult to walk through the trees on her bleeding feet with no idea when the end could be expected. Once Imra reached Lillerem, she planned to find Syndral. Imra allowed her mind to gloss over the fact that she had not spoken to her sister since Syndral deserted from the Dredfall army. For now, Imra focused on the relationship she and her sister had once had.

Imra needed Syndral to know Ulford was dead. This was news that would help Syndral sleep at night on a personal level, not just because Lillerem was safe from Dredfall's former king. Ulford had made it his goal to eliminate all descendants of King Andril. Syndral and her daughter had been in Ulford's crosshairs. The only reason he had not reached Syndral or Riva was because King Blaith's line, including Kindra and the princes, had been his priority. As a member of the Dredfall army, Syndral had known to hide her daughter from Ulford, and now Imra would be able to share the news that Riva was finally safe.

Imra really wanted the reunion with her sister to go well. If she was fortunate, Imra might get to find out what it was like to be an aunt. Riva was her family too, after all. Imra was momentarily overwhelmed by unexpected emotion. Imra had a family. For many years, it had only been Syndral and Imra. When Imra fell in love with Ulford, Syndral had withdrawn from Imra's life. It was not intentional; the two sisters simply did not see each other often as a result of the different stations they held. By the time Syndral deserted, Imra hadn't really felt as if she'd lost a sister. She had just been angry that her own blood had committed the offense.

Imra stopped walking. She held her breath and listened for danger. Her magic was urging her to change direction. It was not a small course correction this time, either. Imra felt the need to turn to her right and find a place to hide. She turned and quickly picked her way through a patch of brambles. The thorns cut into her legs painfully, and she knew they were now bleeding as well. She ducked behind a massive boulder as the scent of rotting fungus filled her nostrils. Imra closed her eyes and felt for changes in her magic. She needed to be ready to move at the slightest nudge from her power.

CHAPTER 8

Riva sat as quietly as she could in the linen closet. She had no idea how one home, even a castle, could ever need so many pillows. The upside was that her hiding spot was extremely comfortable. The closet was about half the size of her old bedroom in New York. There wasn't enough room to set up a bed, but Riva had pulled several of the pillows from the shelves and piled them on the floor to make a little nest. She had been in the closet for over an hour.

As Riva turned the page to begin the next chapter of her book, Mildred's voice sounded from somewhere down the hall. Riva covered her mouth and did her best to keep from giggling. As Mildred moved closer to the linen closet calling Riva's name, Riva heard the doors in the hallway opening and shutting. Mildred was checking for Riva room by room. Riva closed her book. It seemed her brief reprieve from castle life was about to end. A tiny laugh escaped from Riva when Mildred slammed a nearby door shut and cursed. The old female was muttering under her breath when she yanked open the door to the linen closet and found Riva ensconced among the pillows.

"I suppose you think you're amusing?" Mildred asked.

"No, Mam," replied Riva.

"I suppose you are well aware you've missed your history lesson? Are you at least locked away in this closet with a historical text?"

"No, Mam. It's the story of a young maiden who rides —"

Mildred cut Riva off. "Young lady, I have no interest in the drivel you're filling your mind with. Lord Viktor and Lady Ruth pay a lot of coin for you to have excellent tutors in all subjects. You cannot expect to go missing lessons as you see fit without there being any consequences."

"But Mildred!" Riva began, before receiving a stern look from the older female.

Riva tried again. "I don't understand why I can't take my history lessons with Einar, Mam. He knows more about the kingdom than anyone else alive. He lived through all the wars, and he tells the best stories, and it makes history so much more interesting."

Mildred's husband, Einar, had been alive for several hundred years. He had experienced a lot of Lillerem's history first-hand. That did not mean he was a qualified tutor. Einar, now the castle cook, told entertaining stories of the past and was a source of a great deal of historical knowledge, but Einar had opinions. Mildred and the Lord and Lady of the house were in agreement that Riva should receive an unbiased account of the history of Lillerem. Einar's version of history tended to be tainted by his own perceptions of the past and his own opinion of the people who formed it.

"You are not forbidden from indulging in Einar's stories. You get an earful every time you take your meals," said Mildred. "A proper lady is educated in all historical matters, not just those my husband finds important. You will be raised as a proper lady, regardless of the energy you put into avoiding it! Now, pick up those pillows and head to the kitchen. You can peel potatoes for tonight's meal."

The girl scampered off excitedly to the kitchen, leaving the pillows untouched. Mildred was aware she had just given the girl what she wanted. Riva would get her history lesson from Einar while she peeled potatoes. It was going to be an extraordinarily long lesson today. Castle Millspare was expecting more guests than it had seen in months.

Mildred picked the pillows up from the floor, shaking her head. She was far too old to be chasing after children. She had dressed for battle and killed her share of the enemy when Millspare fell under attack less than a year ago, but caring for Riva was wearing Mildred out. Tonight would be better. Riva would have so many people to hold her attention; Mildred would scarcely need to watch the girl. Mildred pulled linens from a shelf and entered a bed-chamber decorated in green and gold. She changed the sheets and laid out clean towels in the bath chamber. She had already done this in six other guest rooms and she had three more rooms to go.

In the kitchen, a wet nose nuzzled Riva's arm as she sat down at the oversized table. She ignored the knife and potatoes waiting in front of her and thrust her hands into the fur of the creature that had silently approached her. Cassidy, the German Shepherd Dog that had been a security blanket for Riva when she had made the adjustment to leaving her foster parents, accepted the love with enthusiasm. Jess Bennett entered the kitchen with her other Shepherd, Butch, at her heels. Jess gave Riva a smile, then went to the stove to accept a hug from Einar. Einar ushered Jess to the table and promptly put out a bowl of fruits and poured Jess some tea.

Jess had been Riva's eighth-grade math teacher in the human realm. She had removed Riva from her foster home to protect the young elf from assassins and hundespor sent to kill anyone with Elven blood. Jess and the princes of Lillerem had moved Riva to Castle Millspare, with Syndral's consent, to prevent Ulford from discovering her.

Jess tossed a berry into the air and deftly caught it in her mouth. Riva suppressed a smile. The young elf understood that Jess was taking a little time to enjoy her Fae form. Humans with Elven blood, such as Jess and Kindra, changed forms when traveling to and from Alfheim. The women were human when in their home-realm, but once they emerged from the portal in Alfheim, they took on a more muscular build and possessed a lot more physical strength and coordination. Both Jess and Kindra reported that they could feel their ears and canine teeth lengthening slightly by the time they were half-way through the portal tunnels.

Riva pulled her face from Cassidy's fluffy neck. "Hey Jess, how long are you staying this time?"

"Not long, Riva. A few days to a few weeks. I am off from school for the summer, but I'm sure Sean will expect his wife back eventually."

Riva bowed her head. "I miss having summers off. Here, they have tutors for me all year. I won't get a break. It's not fair."

Jess refrained from rolling her eyes. "It's my understanding that your tutors only take up about three hours of your precious time each day. Compare that to the seven hours a day you spent in your New York school."

"I'd rather that," said Riva, sticking out her bottom lip.

"Grass, greener, and all that. We always want what we don't have," Jess sighed.

"But I'm all alone here. I have no friends and nobody to talk to except Mildred and Einar," Riva whined.

Jess was not exactly sure how to respond to this complaint. She was pretty sure Riva hadn't had any friends in the human world and that Riva hadn't had anyone to talk to except her parents and a bunch of stuffed animals. That would not be appropriate to point out to Riva, though. Instead, Jess chose to ignore that part of Riva's grievance.

"You're such a lucky girl! Mildred and Einar are two of the nicest people—" Jess caught herself. She didn't need to lie to the girl. "Einar is the sweetest person alive. I bet you love talking to him and listening to his stories. I'm sure Mildred always makes sure you have whatever you need."

"I still hate it here," said Riva.

Jess sighed. "Peel your potatoes, little one. I know you don't believe me, but one day you will realize you hated a lot of things that were actually pretty awesome."

Jess sent a mental command to Butch and Cassidy to remain in the kitchen with Riva. She pushed the dogs a mental image of Riva feeding them little slices of potato under the table to ensure they stayed put. Jess headed off into the depths of Millspare to find Mildred and see if the old female needed any help readying the castle for the evening ahead.

Mildred was in Kindra's chambers when Jess found her. The skin surrounding her eyes crinkled when Jess walked into the room and Mildred walked around the canopied bed to give Jess a hug. Kindra's bedroom always reminded Jess of the room little girls demanded after seeing too many princess movies. She was unsure if any more pink and white could be crammed into one sleeping chamber.

"Jess, always so good to see you. Are Butch and Cassidy in the kitchen?"

"Those dogs are not fools. I'm sure Riva and Einar started sneaking morsels to them the moment I left to find you," replied Jess.

"That child will be the death of me. She is so stubborn! Her mother is still coming this evening, correct?" Mildred asked.

"Syndral will be here any minute, though I am not sure she has much more control over Riva than you do. At this point, you've put more time into raising the girl than Syndral has," replied Jess.

"It's not Syndral's fault entirely," said Mildred. "If Syndral were here more often, it would draw attention and Ulford would be bound to discover Riva was here. It's not a perfect solution, but it has worked well so far."

"I'm going to wash up, and then I'll be down to the kitchen to lend a hand," said Jess.

"Don't bother. Riva skipped her history tutor today. She has been sentenced to potatoes and stories from Einar. Oh! I almost forgot, don't put on any fancy clothes for dinner. Ruth and Viktor are coming down to the kitchen. There will be no formal meal this evening. It's more of a family affair."

Jess raised an eyebrow. It wasn't like the Lord and Lady of the house to pass on an opportunity to put on airs for the local nobility and courtiers. Jess had been looking forward to finding out what color gown her wardrobe would choose for her this evening, but she supposed she could try to get excited about leggings and a tunic instead.

Mildred explained. "A rider arrived about an hour ago from Smalgroth. Ulford lives. Though we will be celebrating Kindra's liberation, I imagine Ruth anticipates the need for plans to be formulated in private. The others arrived in Smalgroth late this morning. They rode through the night, so they'll rest there for a while. We should expect them between six and seven bells."

Jess headed to her chambers. The plan had been to kill Ulford while he sat upon his own throne. The action would not only have removed a cruel slave-owning king from power, but it would draw almost all the soldiers in Dredfall. With the soldiers responding to Ulford's murder, the way would be clear to free Kindra and quickly leave the city. Since Ulford had lived through the attack, Jess imagined her friends would have an interesting story to tell when they arrived at Millspare.

Stepping into her chambers, Jess's first thought was that Mildred had not finished up in this room yet. There were pillows all over the floor. Jess was further confused when she saw there were pillows on the bed as well. Then it hit her. A smile spread across her face. The floor pillows were for Butch and Cassidy. Closer inspection confirmed Jess's theory when she saw the floor pillows were in two separate piles.

Jess went to her wardrobe. Her absolute favorite part of visiting Alfheim was the magical wardrobes that chose clothing for you. Somehow, the furniture read the mind of the user, and combined that information with innate practical knowledge to offer up the exact outfit you needed for an occasion. The darn things even picked fabric in shades that highlighted your eye color and complexion.

Jess pulled open the double doors and withdrew a simple set of dark leggings paired with a beige tunic. Jess smiled when she saw the small purple flowers delicately embroidered down both sides of the tunic. She appreciated the wardrobe's attention to detail. Jess went into the bath chamber to wash her face. Two metal dog dishes containing fresh water sat next to the washbowl. Shaking her head, Jess wondered what personal details Mildred added to the rooms of this evening's other guests.

Jess changed out of her clothes from home and into the tunic and leggings. She sat on the bed and laced her boots. She wanted to call the dogs up to the room and take a nap. Jess was excited to see her friends tonight, but she anticipated there would be work ahead and she was prematurely exhausted. She dragged herself from the bed and forced energy into her body. This was something she was accustomed to doing while teaching. It was important to give her period-nine students the same enthusiasm she gave to the students during the first period of the day. Jess headed for the kitchen to offer her help to Einar.

Einar was performing when Jess returned to the kitchen. Not only was he putting together the meal for the evening, he was embroiled in a story about the crowning of King Andril. Jess had only been a resident of Alfheim for a few months, but she had heard variations of this story from many residents of Lillerem when she had lived here.

"It was not the people who chose Andril, though they liked him just fine," said Einar. "In those days, one was proclaimed king by the Fae of the forest. The people had to abide by their decision. With Andril, a sword named Forsvarer sang to him as a way of making him known to the Fae as a worthy candidate."

Jess, now seated and helping to peel potatoes, interrupted. "That stupid sword sang to Kindra too, and look where it got us."

Einar smiled. "Forsvarer was forged by the Fae of the forest and answers to their will, not ours."

"You should mention that to Kindra," said Jess. "She and Leif talk about that sword as if it is their family heirloom."

"It is, in a way," replied Einar. "Forsvarer alerted the Fae of the forest that Andril would be the best choice for a king. Under Andril's rule, Lillerem was united, strong, and prosperous. Not only was the kingdom successful, but so were the people as individuals. The sword was passed through the generations of kings and eventually sent by Ekkelle to the human realm for safe keeping when she hid her sons there."

"How did Kindra end up with Forsvarer?" asked Riva.

Jess fielded the question. "Kindra was looking for the father she had never known. Once she met Leif, Kindra took a trip to Norway to visit his family home to try to understand him better."

"I'm not sure that is possible when it comes to Leif," said Einar, chuckling.

Jess continued, "Anyway, Kindra was in the garage when Forsvarer started singing to her. It played some melody only she could hear, and the hunk of metal sent Kindra through a portal to this place. The rest is history."

"This is a history lesson," said Einar. "We should fill in some of the details."

"Take it away," said Jess. "I'm just bitter that Kindra's entire life was changed by a sword, and therefore my life was completely changed as well."

"When Forsvarer sang to Kindra, it was only the second time in known history that the sword chose an individual as worthy. When Kindra arrived here at Millspare, we knew she was special," said Einar.

"I don't understand," said Riva. "When the sword sang for Andril, he was crowned king. Why isn't Kindra the king of Lillerem?"

"The name Forsvarer means 'defender', not 'king'," said Einar. "It is thought that the sword can identify the people who will be responsible for saving the Kingdom of Lillerem, but it does not dictate in what capacity that will be. Andril defended Lillerem as its king, but this does not mean Kindra must do it the same way."

"So, Kindra could still be the King of Lillerem one day?" Riva asked.

"Something like that," replied Einar. "You never know what will happen in the future. To date, all the kings of Lillerem have been male, but that does not mean it needs to stay that way forever."

CHAPTER 9

Alek was not sure what he was supposed to do. When the wagon had entered Smalgroth, he had watched in wonder as the sights rolled past him. The merchant cart had stopped in front of a small house with a covered front porch. Everyone had stepped from the wagon. Krish and Bane had headed straight for the stables. Gunnar, riding in the front of the wagon with Frida, had told the group he would see them shortly and left with Frida when she drove the wagon down the road. Alek was now sitting on a wooden fence, wondering what was supposed to come next.

Alek had hoped to speak to Frida once the wagon stopped. He was not sure why he found the female so intriguing. Maybe it was simply because she was the only one in the group he had not had a chance to speak with. Alek was certain it was not a budding interest in leather tooling. Frida's craftsmanship was impressive, but Alek could not imagine sitting around all day at a bench. He really needed some space to move around. Actually, he had been cooped up in that wagon for over twelve hours, and the need to expel some energy had his insides buzzing.

When Kindra, Joral, Leif and Trego entered the house with the porch, Alek was alone in the street. He pushed off the fence and landed deftly on his feet. Jogging off in the direction Frida had driven the wagon, Alek went down each side street as he used up some of his pent-up energy. Little shops lined most of the streets and it looked as if the people who owned them lived in the upstairs rooms. Alek eventually slowed to a walk so he could look into the windows of the shops. He was curious what each place sold and the signs announcing that information were useless to an Elven child who did not know his letters.

It had been exceptionally tricky to hide his inability to read from Kindra. He had shared with her that his favorite place to sneak off and visit in the city of Fallholm was the library. When Alek saw Kindra's face light up at the mention of the word, he had tried to backtrack and explain that it wasn't really a library and that it was just a warehouse with boxes of books. Unfortunately, the thought of a huge facility full of forgotten books got Kindra even more excited. Alek had retrieved ink and paper for Kindra so she could write down the exact things Alek should look for in the titles under the pretense of being afraid he might forget them. Kindra must have been just as worried as Alek pretended to be, because she wrote down a lot of words for him each time. Instead of reading the titles of books in the warehouse, Alek had matched words in the titles to words on Kindra's list.

Alek was back on the main street now, and he smelled leather. He held his hands up to the window next to him to cut down on the glare and peered inside. It was definitely the leather shop. Alek followed the side of the building down a small alley and found his way to the back. There was a stairway leading to a small porch and a door on the second floor. Frida's wagon was parked behind Alek. Knowing nothing of etiquette, Alek mounted the steps to go and rap on the door.

Just before Alek announced his presence with a knock, he heard voices and stopped; closed fist poised in front of the door. Frida and Gunnar must have been sitting just inside the entrance, because Alek could hear the conversation clearly.

Frida said, "I just don't know what it is about the child. I am drawn to him, but it is almost as if I am afraid to speak to him."

"You're afraid of a child?" asked Gunnar.

"Well, no. I'm not afraid of him. It is as if I can sense that speaking to him will change things. It's like I already know I am going to learn something I don't want to know."

Gunnar snorted. "You're starting to sound like a crazy old female. Would you care to consult some tea leaves before continuing your prophecy?"

"It's not funny, Gunnar. Haven't you ever felt a sense of being on the edge of change? It's not exactly foreboding, but I feel something."

"Yes. I felt that way just before I lost you," said Gunnar.

"You never lost me. We just grew apart. We were both busy. It was no one's fault."

"Yet, I felt it before it ever happened. I didn't know what it was at the time, but now I know it was the sense that something important was slipping away from me," Gunnar said.

Alek turned from the door and went back down the stairs. He sat on the bottom step, uncertain about what he should do. Alek knew he felt a pull toward Frida, but his feelings had not seemed bad in any way. The things Frida had been saying to Gunnar made it sound as if the female had a bad feeling about him. *Am I bad? Would these people be better off without me around?*

When Alek fled Dredfall on the top of the wagon, he had not been thinking about what would happen to him. He had only known he needed to get away. As his adventure was unfolding, Alek had started thinking of himself as part of this little group of travelers, but he wasn't. Alek was completely alone, with nowhere to live and no way to provide for himself. Hours ago, Alek had been elated to escape a life of bondage that would inevitably end in an early death. His only thought had been to get away from Skilanis. He had even felt he might be able to return to Dredfall and help end slavery there. Alek's fantasies were disintegrating in the face of his current reality.

The door above Alek swung open, and the young elf whipped his head up and around to face the sound. Gunnar stepped from the house. The warrior stopped mid-stride and stared down at Alek. Alek stood and started backing away from Frida's home.

"I'm sorry, Gunnar. I didn't know where to go. Everyone kinda went off to their own places and I didn't know what to do or who I should go with... or if I should go with anyone, ya know? I just, um...I just kinda went off in the direction you and Frida went and I was looking in the shops. I uh... I ended up here. I smelled the leather, ya know?"

Gunnar held up a hand to stop Alek's babbling. He ran a hand through his hair and shifted on his feet. He looked from the door behind him to the young elf standing a few feet from the foot of the stairs.

"Apparently, Alek, you belong here. I was pretty surprised to see you, but not unhappy. Frida just sent me out to find you… and here you are."

The grin on Alek's face could be no bigger. The boy's eyes were wide with excitement. Gunnar felt as if he were standing next to explosives. Frida had been full of trepidation when she decided she wanted to put her feelings about Alek to rest and just speak to the boy. Alek, on the other hand, looked as if Gunnar had just told him he could have ice cream for breakfast. Gunnar was not looking forward to witnessing the meeting of these elves. Slowly, Gunnar turned back around and went into the house. He left the door ajar for Alek to follow him in.

Alek paused for only a second before bounding up the stairs and stepping through the doorway. He closed the door behind him and found Frida and Gunnar seated at a small kitchen table. Alek sat down in the chair directly in front of him, staring at Frida, who was seated on the other side of the square table. Something inside of his body tickled. It was as if his very blood was excited to be sitting in this tiny kitchen. He tried to keep his hands still in his lap, and his right leg was bouncing under the table. Alek felt as if he needed to speak, but words were escaping him. He wanted to get up and go touch Frida; shake her hand, or hug her. Never, in all his years, had Alek ever experienced the kind of anxious excitement he was feeling right now.

At last, Alek managed a few slow breaths and was able to focus on Frida. She was pale. Her white skin made the freckles on her nose stand out and made the tinge of green more obvious in her completion. The female did not look well and Alek started adjusting his position so he was not directly across from Frida. He need not have worried. Frida suddenly stood and ran from the room with her hand over her mouth. Alek looked at Gunnar for an explanation, but the male simply shrugged.

"Should I go make sure she is ok?" Alek asked.

"I expect she'll be back when she is ready. Maybe you should just wait here."

The wait seemed longer than it was. Alek and sat at the table with Gunnar. He tried to engage the male in conversation, but gave up when Gunnar only responded with disinterested, single-word answers. When Frida reemerged five minutes later, she announced her presence by taking a deep breath before entering the room. Her eyes were slightly red, and she was stiff as she walked to the table. She sat down and released the breath she had been holding.

"I think I need to tell you both a story," Frida began. "Almost forty-one summers ago, I was very involved in taking care of my aging mother. As Gunnar knows, it took up nearly all of my time. She eventually passed on, but for years, she was my only concern. I rid myself of all other obligations and responsibilities. I no longer kept up with friends or... those who were more than friends."

Frida looked at Gunnar. He placed his hand on the table and Frida placed her hand on top of his. She gave the back of Gunnar's hand a little squeeze and then continued with her story.

"One of the responsibilities I did not have the time for was caring for a baby."

Gunnar's arm stiffened visibly, and then he dragged his hand back. Alek watched the motion and felt he understood what Frida was about to explain to Gunnar, but she had stopped speaking. Gunnar stared at Frida. Alek saw a bunch of emotions cross the warrior's face. He recognized anger and sadness, but he was unfamiliar with the others.

"What did you do?" Gunnar asked. "Why didn't you tell me?"

Frida was looking at Gunnar when she said, "You were busy, too. Ulford had declared war on Lillerem and was carving a swath of the kingdom for himself. You were needed on the front lines and only just getting to know your own family after having spent your childhood in the human realm and away from Alfheim. I could not expect you to help me."

"Things might have been so different..." Gunnar let his thought trail off. He focused on Frida. "I had a right to know. What did you do? What happened to the child?"

Frida slowly moved her gaze from Gunnar to Alek. Alek smiled back at the female. He was hanging on to the edge of his seat, wondering what happened to her baby.

"How can you possibly know that?" Gunnar asked.

Alek was confused. Had he zoned out and missed the part where Frida explained what had happened to the baby?

Gunnar's eyes were roving over Alek in a way they had not done before. He froze when Alek met his stare. The golden eyes looking back at Gunnar were familiar. It had been years since he'd seen eyes like that without the weight of the world within their gaze, but Gunnar knew those eyes.

Still looking at Alek, Frida continued her story. "I gave birth to you on my own. I had no help. The neighbor heard my screams and broke into my house, thinking I was under attack. Once he saw I was in labor, he went and stayed in the kitchen. I called to him once you were born. He cut your cord and cleaned you up. I asked him to help me. He promised me he would take you to a good home. He told me he knew a woman who wanted a baby."

Frida was crying openly at this point and her story was dissolving into a puddle of words that were increasingly difficult to understand. Alek, finally realizing what had happened to the baby, looked back and forth between Frida and Gunnar. He saw Frida's freckles. He saw Gunnar's eyes. He felt a new feeling boiling up to the surface. The nervous energy from earlier was being replaced with a surge of anger like he had never felt before.

The dishes, drying in the rack by the basin, lifted into the air, sailed across the room and smashed into the wall. Alek pushed back from the table, hard. The table bumped into Frida, but Alek did not care. He turned and left the house. He ran down the steps and straight across the tiny yard to the wagon. Shutting himself inside it, Alek sat in the middle of the floor and pulled his knees up to his chest. Strangely, this little space on the wooden planks was soothing. What did it say about the direction his life had taken that Alek felt more comfortable on the floor of a wagon than anywhere else?

The door to the wagon opened and the entire carriage rocked to one side as Gunnar entered and took a seat on a wooden bench. Alek watched as the usually stoic warrior crumpled into the seat. Gunnar placed his elbows on his knees and rested his head in his hands. The two males sat there silently; a merchant cart full of anger and confusion.

"Well, at least you know where you belong now," said Gunnar.

Alek's eyebrows met in the center of his forehead. He looked disbelievingly at Gunnar.

"Where I belong? Maybe once, but my mother gave me away. How can I belong with her?"

"You could also be alone. From experience, I don't think you would enjoy that as much. She's confused right now too, but I suspect you need each other," Gunnar appealed to Alek.

"What about you? Frida lied to you. You didn't see each other for years, then she didn't even tell you about me when she saw you again. Are you going to go back into her kitchen and be her friend again?" asked Alek.

"Point taken. You know what we need? Food. I'm thinking we should go visit my friend Kanin. He will have food you never knew you wanted to eat," said Gunnar.

"What's so great about his food?" asked Alek.

"Kanin Gundersen farms food from the human realm for the King of Lillerem. King Erik is very particular about his vegetables. The King finds the traditional greens found here in Lillerem to be too bland and imports seeds from the human realm to be grown in Smalgroth. Would you like to give it a try?"

"What I'd really like right now is to skip the food and go straight to the human realm," Alek gave Gunnar a small smile.

Gunnar gently flicked Alek's pointed ear. "Trust me, kiddo, you wouldn't find things much easier there."

Without waiting for Alek to make a decision, Gunnar stood and exited the wagon. Gunnar had not made it around the house to the main road before Alek caught up and kept pace beside him. Several minutes later, Gunnar directed Alek up the few steps of the house with the wooden porch. Alek walked through the door to see Krish and Bane had joined the rest of the group around the table for a snack. The snack looked more like art spread across the table in bowls filled with vegetables of every color.

Gunnar pulled out a chair from beneath the immense table and indicated to Alek that he should have a seat. He walked around the table piling a little of every food onto a plate, then slid the dish in front of Alek. As Alek rolled a cherry tomato around his plate, trying to figure out how to successfully spear it with a fork, everyone else stared at Gunnar. Gunnar, as would be expected, ignored them and served himself. He then took the seat beside Alek.

"So, Alek, what are some things you enjoy doing?" Gunnar asked the young elf.

Alek, discovering olives have pits and withdrawing the hard nodule from his mouth with his fingers, flashed Gunnar a huge grin.

"What I really love is football! Me and the other kids at the barracks play a lot. I'm really good at scoring goals even though I'm not as fast as some of the other kids. It might be because I can use some magic to move the ball into the net, but I don't think too many of the kids notice when I steer the ball a little."

While Alek continued animatedly about football, which Kindra had determined to be soccer, Kindra watched Gunnar. The warrior had not only initiated small-talk with the boy, but Gunnar was smiling as he listened to Alek's responses. When Alek's commentary petered out and Kindra felt she knew more about life in the children's slave barracks than she ever wanted to hear, she confronted Gunnar.

"What's happened since I last saw you two?" Kindra asked.

Gunnar swung his attention to Kindra. There was an almost goofy grin on his face that looked so out of place, Kindra wondered if the male was possessed by the spirit of a matronly kindergarten teacher. Thankfully, Gunnar's usual stoic expression returned within a few seconds of looking away from Alek.

"What happened? Well, I went to Frida's for a bit, and then Alek and I came back here to get some of the best food in Alfheim. Isn't that right, kiddo?" Gunnar looked at Alek for the last part.

Kindra stared at Gunnar. "Kiddo? Who are you, and what have you done with my uncle? My uncle, who does not smile, has no interest in anyone's hobbies, and certainly does not use the word 'kiddo'."

Gunnar glared at Kindra, and Kindra actually felt a little better. The response was much more typical of Gunnar's personality and behaviors. Kindra stole a glance at the others around the table. Leif, Krish, Joral and Bane looked as concerned as Kindra felt. Kanin and Alek were involved in a heated debate about the differences in the fresh greens on the table. Alek was unimpressed with the taste of the collard greens, and Kanin had suggested Alek try the Swiss chard instead. Alek argued that it was still just leaves, and he hadn't liked the first batch.

Kindra decided to switch her tactic. "Alek, where did you get off to after we pulled into Smalgroth?"

Alek stopped arguing with Kanin to answer. "You all seemed pretty busy, so I decided to go exploring. I went and found Frida's house. I was going to knock, but Gunnar ended up coming out to find me because Frida wanted to tell me I'm her son."

Kindra dropped her fork onto her plate. Alek reached across the table to grab another helping of carrots drenched in a brown sugar marinade. All eyes but Alek's turned to look at Gunnar. Gunnar grabbed a piece of corn on the cob and slathered it with butter. He took a bite and chewed, without meeting anyone's gaze. He placed the cob down on his plate, wiped his hands, and looked up at last.

"I almost forgot to mention that," Gunnar said. "It appears I have a son."

CHAPTER 10

Syndral sauntered into the Millspare kitchen, projecting more confidence than she felt. She paused for a moment just in case Riva decided to run to her and give her a hug. The little girl did not look up from her potatoes, but Jess offered a cheery smile and a wave. Syndral buried her disappointment and approached the table. Butch sprang to his feet and placed himself between Syndral and her destination.

"Oh yeah," said Syndral. "I forgot how much you adore me."

The dog replied by peeling back his lips to show Syndral the tips of his teeth. Syndral glared at Jess. Jess gave a mock pout, then called Butch back to the table. Butch turned and retreated, but glanced over his shoulder twice before lying down. Syndral sat at the table and picked up a knife to help with the potatoes.

"It's a shame," said Jess.

"What is?" asked Syndral.

"You should have allowed me to let Butch play guardian a little longer. I think he's getting a little soft. You and Leif really bring out his protective nature."

"Your dog has an interest in eating me, and you see it as training. Sometimes you scare me, Jess. How about we work on getting Butch to leave me out of the training sessions and he can focus on Leif from now on?"

"I'll consider it, but Butch has his own mind. You might have to feed him a lot of table scraps before he agrees with the plan," laughed Jess.

Riva sat straight up and slammed her peeling knife down on the table. Jess and Syndral stopped in the middle of their conversation to look at her. Riva's young elf ears were infinitely more sensitive than any adult set of ears. Butch and Cassidy came to attention next, and Jess stretched her mind into theirs in order to listen in on what the dogs were hearing.

"It's a wagon," Jess announced to Syndral and Einar. "They're here!"

Riva was rising from her seat at the table when Syndral threw her a death glare.

"Potatoes?" Syndral asked Riva.

"Almost done," Riva answered.

"Ok," said Syndral. "Finish up and bring them to Einar. No one is going to be happy to see you if they find out the food isn't ready because you didn't take the time to finish peeling the potatoes."

Riva didn't get the chance to greet the new arrivals at the stable. Bane, as usual, was the first to enter the kitchen. He came through the servants' entrance with Joral at his heels. Both males inhaled deeply when they entered the room and sent Einar appreciative looks. Butch blocked Bane and Joral's progress to the table for a moment while he gave them a proper sniff to be sure all was well with the males. Satisfied, Butch allowed them to continue on and sit down. Riva and Syndral greeted the warriors, and Cassidy shifted so the new table guests could pet him.

Jess was about to ask Joral about the journey when Butch growled. His hackles were up and he was staring at the door through which Bane and Joral had just entered. Riva shot from her seat and ran toward the door.

"Uncle Leif!" the girl squealed as she put herself between Butch and the empty doorway.

As soon as Riva was in position, a booted foot poked around the corner, followed by a muscled leg clad in cargo pants from the human realm. Riva started giggling. Butch was still growling. Jess could have had Butch stand down, but she had already cut Butch's intolerance for Syndral short and wanted to allow the dog a little fun. Kindra's father had a prickly personality, and Jess felt he and Butch would be a perfect match if Butch could get over wanting to tear parts of Leif off for use as a snack. Since it didn't seem likely that today would be the day, Jess enjoyed the moment.

"Riva, darling!" called Leif. "Tell me you have that evil beast restrained, and it is safe for me to enter."

Still giggling, Riva replied, "It's safe. You can come in."

Leif stepped the rest of the way through the door. Riva went to the male and gave him a hug. Giving Butch a wide berth, Riva walked Leif over to the table. The girl kept herself between Leif and Butch the entire time. Jess and Syndral were enthralled by Riva's actions for different reasons. Jess could not imagine why the girl was so enamored with Leif. Syndral was amazed that her daughter had absolutely no fear of the snarling canine baring its teeth as Riva glided by with Leif at her side, but she was hurt that Riva was more inclined to run to Leif's rescue than protect her own mother.

Kindra and Krish entered the room next. Walking in with their arms linked, Leif couldn't help himself. He started humming 'Here Comes the Bride' as the two strode toward the table. It was Jess's turn to jump up from the table in delight. Her best friend was free! When Kindra had disappeared weeks earlier, Jess had known something was wrong. The two friends never went more than twenty-four hours without speaking unless there was an excellent reason.

Even Cassidy got up from under the table to greet Kindra. Jess only stopped hugging Kindra because Butch and Cassidy's nails were digging into the women's arms as the dogs tried to become part of the hug. Kindra took one of the two seats closest to the head of the table, and Krish took the one on the opposite side. Though this was not a formal dinner, it would be expected that the future King and Queen of Lillerem had the seats nearest to the Lord and Lady of the house. It was rare for Viktor and Ruth to eat in the kitchen. Even though many of the formalities would be forgotten by taking the meal down here, some traditions would need to be upheld.

"How was the journey?" Syndral asked no one in particular.

Joral responded. "It turned out that getting Kindra out of her cage was easy. That part of the plan went smoothly. Unfortunately, Ulford lives. Imra knew we were coming and ensured Ulford was not in the throne room when we attacked."

"Well, that is... disappointing," Jess said. "Foolishly, I thought this would be the end and we could begin the 'happily ever after' part of the story."

"You really live in a Fairy Tale, don't you?" asked Leif. "There is never a 'happily ever after'. This is real life and there is always someone trying to take power, trying to gain more land, or trying to kill us. You really need to get your head out of your—"

A bread roll hit Leif between the eyes. Syndral was fast. He had not noticed when she grabbed the bread from the basket on the table, but Leif saw the warning in Syndral's eyes. She moved her gaze to Riva to remind Leif that he needed to watch his language.

"Oh, that is rich," said Leif. "Since when did you decide to become a parent?"

"I've always done what is best for Riva! In this case, having someone else raise her was the best option. If anyone should understand that, it's you," said Syndral.

Jess was thoroughly amused by the conversation between Leif and Syndral; neither elf was in line for parent of the year. Syndral had given Riva up for adoption and allowed a very nice human couple to raise her. It sounded kind on the surface, but because of the slow rate at which elves age, the adoption required Riva's human parents to pack up their entire lives and move to another part of the country every few years. Leif, on the other hand, had been completely absent from Kindra's life. Kindra's mother had told Leif to stay away, and he had exchanged his rights as a parent for the right to name his daughter, and then washed his hands of her. Jess didn't know if it was more amusing that Leif was the one calling Syndral out on her parenting skills or if it was Syndral trying to shield Riva from Leif's language. Either way, Jess knew it was unwise to let the two of them fight it out in front of Riva.

"Oh man! It is so good to see you, Kindra!" Jess exclaimed. "How on earth did you survive captivity?"

Kindra smiled, understanding the need for a shift in conversation. "Funny you should ask that question... I had help. The comical part is that the help seems to have hitched a ride with us and is here at Millspare. I expect he'll be along shortly with Trego and Gunnar. My new little buddy wanted to meet all the horses."

"Did you bring home a dog from the kennels?" Jess demanded. "How could you fail to tell me that immediately?"

"No, not a dog at all. I was kind of hoping Riva might enjoy meeting my new companion, but seeing that Syndral has suddenly become a little overprotective, I'm not so sure anymore."

"If this is your new companion, why aren't you out there showing off the horses?" Jess asked.

"Let's just say that absent parents are becoming a theme lately," replied Kindra.

Mildred entered the kitchen. "Riva dear, run quick and get the others from the stable. Lord Viktor and Lady Ruth are on their way down."

Riva was off with no questions asked. Mildred and Einar bustled around the kitchen, stepping over Butch or Cassidy when necessary to be sure the appetizers were ready to be served as soon as the Lord and Lady were seated. Trego strode through the main entrance to the kitchen. Instead of remaining in the stables, he must have entered the castle to greet the Lord and Lady upon his arrival. It was probably a good thing that at least one of them was keeping with local customs. Riva re-entered the kitchen through the servant's door, dragging Alek behind her. The poor kid looked petrified and awestruck simultaneously. Riva pulled Alek down into the seat beside her at the table as Gunnar came through the door and found his own seat.

As if the pair had been waiting just outside of the kitchen until everyone was ready, Lord Viktor and Lady Ruth entered through the main door, arm in arm. Viktor guided his wife to one of the two seats at the head of the table and then claimed the other as his own. Lord Viktor's eyes met everyone else's in turn as if he were taking stock. His survey stalled on Alek. The small boy was the only person at the table who was new to Millspare. Gunnar climbed to his feet.

"Lord Viktor, Lady Ruth, allow me to present my son, Alek."

Riva pinched Alek to make him stand. Alek gave an awkward bow in greeting to the heads of the castle. Lady Ruth was the first to regain her composure. After looking from Alek to Gunnar, and pausing to be sure there wasn't a joke at her expense, she addressed Gunnar.

"First of all, brother, we agreed to hold the meal in the kitchen so we could dispense with the formalities. Feel free to skip the titles. Secondly, while I am pleased to add Alek to our family, I would like a little more detail about when I most recently became an auntie. Did you adopt the child before or after you entered Dredfall to rescue Kindra?"

Alek, still standing, lacked his father's quiet and impassive demeanor. He took it upon himself to explain to the Lady of the house how he came to be a part of the group now sitting at the kitchen table in Castle Millspare. It took several minutes for him to relay how he had hidden on the roof of Frida's wagon, followed Gunnar and Frida to the leather shop, and listened to Frida tell the tale of giving him up. Ruth's expression mirrored Gunnar's usual stoicism as Alek told his story.

"You really can't blame my dad. He didn't know I was his kid, either. Frida was the one who didn't want me and that's how I ended up as a slave. It'll be ok though. My dad told me I can live here and be Riva's friend," finished Alek.

The corner of Ruth's mouth twitched, but her blue eyes were icy. Alek sat down slowly under her glare. He no longer looked as confident as he had been a moment earlier. Riva looked as if she were bubbling with excitement, but she knew better than to let it show, so she was doing her best to keep the energy wrapped up beneath her skin.

"So, my brother told you that you could live here, did he?" Ruth said the words to Alek, but they were also meant for Gunnar.

Alek flashed a winning smile in Ruth's direction. His curly hair flopped down over his eyes at the perfect time to be adorably cute. Alek pushed his hair back, revealing the freckles across the bridge of his nose, and waited expectantly to hear what Ruth would say next.

Ruth stared into Alek's golden eyes and could no longer hold her composure. Her eyes softened, and a smile caused them to crinkle at the corners. She stood from the table, and completely forgoing any propriety, went to throw her arms around Gunnar.

"You're a father! I'm an aunt! Our family lives on!" Ruth said with joy.

Gunnar, still sitting, reached up to pat his elder sister on the shoulder. His mouth was pressed into a line as he waited for the emotional part of the announcement to pass. Kindra cleared her throat and Gunnar relaxed a little.

"Excuse me! I do believe you already found out you were an aunt a few months ago!" Kindra said, pretending to be hurt.

Ruth, replied serenely, "It's just not the same being an aunt to someone your age."

With the tense moment passed, food started to make its way to the table. Mildred stopped in the middle of serving squash to give Alek an appraising look. The boy would only begin to know what it meant to be a part of the family, and under Mildred's scrutiny, after the meal. Unlike a formal meal, Mildred and Einar joined the group at the table and the discussion revolved around the tale of Kindra's rescue and fighting off Skilanis's beasts in the Dredskog.

Alek proudly relayed all he knew about the hundespor, frost giants, merknifol and langen the group had encountered in the forest. Syndral nodded along until he described the frost giants. She held up her hand for Alek to stop.

"He sent frost giants after you?" Syndral questioned. "That doesn't make any sense. It's too warm for them here. They would not be able to move quickly enough to have caught you in the forest. They must have been there before you even attempted an attack on Castle Bindrell. The hundespor hunt in the forest in the evenings, but Skilanis never lets his other monsters roam free."

"That's not entirely true," Krish cut in. "Months ago, we were attacked by mist creatures. What did you call them, Alek? Merknifol?"

Alek nodded enthusiastically. He was bursting with pride at being helpful.

Krish continued. "At the time, we had never seen them before. We were sleeping around a fire in the woods outside of Millspare when we woke to the potent scent of mushrooms."

"If I recall, that was the night we found out how well Kindra held a sword," said Gunnar.

Hiding a smile, Joral added, "That was all she did, if I remember correctly. She held her sword in a fighting stance and just froze there."

"That is not fair!" Kindra exclaimed. "At that point, all Gunnar had taught me was how to take up a stance!"

"Stop!" Syndral raised her voice. "Are you telling me that the merknifol were not only outside of Fallholm but within Lillerem's borders?"

Viktor said, "We were regularly experiencing incursion by Dredfall troops. On that evening, we fled into the woods to escape a foray by a band of enemy soldiers. The castle was defended safely, but we encountered the mist creatures while hiding in the wooded lands attached to the city of Aergroth. Honestly, we knew the creatures were not of this realm, and were unsure if they were related to Dredfall's attack, but we did nothing to further investigate the creatures. There had been no complaints from villagers about them and we never chanced upon them again until now. Why is the presence of these creatures in Lillerem so significant?"

"I'm surprised, but not completely sure of the significance," said Syndral. "The information Alek has shared with you about the variety of Skilanis's creatures and their abilities is not a secret. The part that is not common knowledge is that Ulford imposed a set of rules on Skilanis regarding his pets staying within the city walls. The most important rule was that the creatures would not be permitted to harm city residents, including slaves. It is the primary reason the hundespor leave Fallholm for the Dredskog when they hunt.

"The second rule imposed on Skilanis and his pets was that all creatures of the darker realms must remain within the borders of Dredfall. I assume Ulford's directive to use hundespor in the human realm must have eliminated, or at least modified, that second rule, but you encountered the merknifol prior to Ulford sanctioning the use of the hundespor."

It was Ruth's turn to speak. "I'm not sure why that is significant. Maybe Ulford had previously sanctioned the use of Skilanis's creatures and you were unaware?"

"No," replied Syndral. "It was not a negotiable rule. I was still leading Dredfall's Second Draw at the time. Use of Skilanis's creatures would have ensured our ability to take Castle Millspare. Ulford refused to let us use any of the creatures because he is petrified of them. Only Skilanis has some semblance of control over his pets. If those creatures were outside of Dredfall, they were either there of their own accord, or Skilanis was using them in direct opposition to Ulford's orders. Frankly, I'm not sure which scenario is more disturbing."

Alek offered some insight. "I have worked in the kennels for over twenty years. Other than the hundespor, the creatures do not roam freely. They must be released from the cages. Skilanis conjures the merknifol from Niflheim when he goes out into the Dredskog. Tobias, the houndsman, and I would help lock the creatures up when Skilanis returned. What if Skilanis wasn't bringing them all back with him?"

"Exactly," said Syndral. "What if Skilanis has been pushing his own agenda?"

"That is… unsettling," said Krish. "As terrible as Ulford is, he is relatively predictable. It was almost comforting to know that Ulford's underlings were no more than weapons Ulford used in attempts to further his objectives. Knowing Skilanis might have an alternative goal and that he would act on it without fear of repercussion from Ulford…" Krish stopped speaking aloud as his thoughts undoubtedly drifted to increasingly scary scenarios.

Alek watched each person around the table. He had known Kindra the longest, and she looked more distressed during this conversation than she had ever appeared during the entire time of her captivity. He looked at Gunnar next. Alek was now calling him 'father' when speaking out loud, but he was still coming to terms with having a dad. The warrior was unique and intriguing. Alek admitted to himself that he was excited about this male being his father.

Gunnar sat through the entire conversation impassively. Alek watched closely for any sign of emotion on the warrior's face, but he detected none. It was Gunnar's looks that made him an enigma. Closing his eyes, Alek felt emotion emanating from Gunnar. The emotion was there, constantly roiling just under the skin, but it was completely invisible. Alek wasn't sure if he could feel it because Gunnar was his father, or if everyone could feel it, if they were willing to allow senses other than sight to take Gunnar in. Likely, it was subconscious. It didn't seem like a single person held any ill-will toward Gunnar, despite his seemingly distant personality. It was as if people just knew Gunnar was a solid source of support for those in need.

Alek turned his attention to Leif. Like Gunnar, Leif portrayed an air of indifference. That might be the only similarity between the brothers. No warmth emanated from Leif. The only person Leif cared about was Leif. Alek had heard about Leif's return to Alfheim on account of Kindra being here, but Kindra was his daughter. Leif viewed Kindra as an extension of himself. The need to protect her and the pride he felt were not a result of Kindra's actions or accomplishments.

As the conversation continued around the table, Alek focused his senses on the Lord and Lady. Viktor and Ruth were the picture of nobility. Once again, the vision did not match what Alek felt from them. Viktor felt insecure. He ruled Aergroth in name only. He deferred to his wife. Ruth loathed her position as the lady by his side.

It wasn't Viktor causing her to feel that way. Ruth loved him. It was the power she detested.

Suddenly Alek stopped thinking. He opened his eyes and tried to focus on the surrounding conversation. Talk had started about a return trip to Dredfall to finish off Ulford, but those around the table were unsure how to address Skilanis now that he stood revealed as a major threat in the shadow of Ulford's throne. Alek couldn't focus. The veil of denial was slipping. He knew no one else at the table could do what he was doing. At last, Alek accepted that he was able to feel the emotions of the others. *I guess I have more power than I thought.*

CHAPTER 11

Imra ducked off the main path and found a spot behind a boulder to wait. She had been making her way through the Dredskog for hours. Relying heavily on her power of premonition was steadily wearing down her strength, and she was grateful for the respite, even though her heart was in her throat. There was no sound as she watched the frost giants lumber past her position. The first time this had happened, she foolishly left her hiding place too soon. This time, she remained hidden. In the daylight, the merknifol were not a problem, but Imra had discovered that the langen always followed closely behind the frost giants. The langen hunted by detecting heat. Remaining still and silent in her location, Imra hoped her heat signature had already dissipated and the ophidian creatures would not be able to see the path she had taken into the brush.

After a moment, she heard it. The slithering sound came, not just from the ground, but from the branches above the trail Imra had been traversing moments ago. She waited for the sound to die out completely, and then walked off to the south, forgoing the trail entirely. Imra had hoped to be out of the dark forest by now, but patrols of Skilanis's unnatural beings kept causing her to take cover and lose time. Progress through the Dredskog was sluggish. Imra felt the monsters were searching for something. She was sure her sensory gift had steered her to choose the path of the frost giants, as opposed to a direction teeming with hundespor. Those beasts would have scented her before she had barely trekked half-way through the forest. The most pressing issue right now was the setting sun. Imra needed to get out of the woods before the merknifol joined the patrols.

Imra was a powerful seeress. Her magic allowed her to remain out of harm's way. This did not make Imra invincible. Like the rest of Ulford's Elite Guard, Imra was trained in hand-to-hand combat, but she had never excelled at it in the way the others had. If not for her particular gifts, Ulford would have never even taken an interest in her.

It was Imra's power, combined with her desire to keep Ulford alive, that had steered Imra to prevent Ulford from being in the throne room last evening. Imra couldn't understand why she had not been aware that Skilanis would betray them. An idea formed in her mind and took hold. The only explanation was that protecting Ulford against Skilanis would have meant her own death.

Imra pulled the plain dress supplied to her by Tomia from a pricker-bush. If not for the dress, the encounter with the older female might have been a dream. This morning, when there had been no other evidence that the woman lived in the tiny shack at all, Imra's mind had spun out of control trying to explain the night's events. Now Imra was just happy she was no longer in a gown. She would deal with her thoughts about the strange woman once she found safety.

Imra broke from the tree-line and into the rolling fields that marked the outskirts of Lillerem. She was unsure exactly where she was along the border between kingdoms, but she knew Millspare would not be far. The dense growth of the forest she had pushed through for her entire journey was a sign she had been on the shortest route from Fallholm to Aergroth. Now, she just needed to find a road or a farm; anything to help her get her bearings.

Imra walked along the edge of the forest. She would have to come across someone at some point. It was natural that there were no homes this close to the border with Dredfall, but Imra knew there were people living within a few miles of the border between the kingdoms. Imra stumbled and fell to her hands and knees. The adrenaline from evading the creatures in the Dredskog had leached away and exhaustion set in. She let herself fall to the earth and she lay in the grass. A fly landed on her hand and she did not even move to swat it away.

"It probably would've been a good idea to bring some water with you on your journey," a familiar voice came from Imra's left.

Water was certainly an issue. Imra knew she was thirsty, but lack of water was now causing her to hallucinate. Things were much direr than she had let herself believe. Imra rolled her head toward the voice, even though she knew she was alone in the field. Sitting on a rock, about a foot from Imra's shoulder, was Tomia. It was possible the rock had been there the whole time, but Imra could not pretend she had simply missed the female's presence before collapsing in exhaustion. Tomia, as if knowing now was the moment to prove she was real, handed Imra a water skin.

"Why are you helping me?" Imra asked after taking a long pull from the skin.

"That's the question you chose to lead with? I figured that one would be a little lower on the list. Are you not more concerned with how I found you or how I seemed to appear out of nowhere?"

"I have my suspicions about that and I honestly don't think I'm ready to have them confirmed. I really just want to know why you are choosing to help me," said Imra.

"You assume I am helping you by choice?" Imra laughed. "Maybe I'm at the mercy of some higher power or something."

"Fine," Imra conceded. "I'll rephrase my question and simply ask why you are helping me."

"I forget how self-centered beings of some realms can be. I am not helping you, Imra. I am preventing the end of all things. For millennia, the realms have been balanced. Recent events, and events to come, threaten the stability I have always maintained. You are a pawn."

If Imra were not so tired, she would have burned some energy to look affronted. Imra had been thinking of Tomia as a protector or some kind of guide, possibly even the personification of her own power of premonition and self-preservation. *Maybe I have been a little self-centered?* Tomia was not looking to help Imra. Her life was being protected solely so Imra could be of aid to Tomia.

Tomia continued. "Now that you have concluded that it is not important to understand why I am helping you, we can move to the part where you accept my help. This will ensure that I can maintain balance. I know you intend to go to your sister for help. That is good.

It is imperative that she and her friends know what has happened so they can better prepare."

"That is the plan," Imra replied. "I was on my way to Millspare when my body decided it didn't agree with the plan."

"Skilanis needs to be stopped," Tomia said. "He has dabbled with the unnatural before, but his current plans ensure the destruction of Alfheim—even if he does not forsee it. If Alfheim is destroyed, balance will be lost, and the other realms will fall as well."

Imra lifted herself up into a seated position. She crossed her legs in front of her and took in the occupant of the rock beside her. Tomia looked like an elf, but even in Imra's state of extreme fatigue, she knew Tomia was other-worldly. Something about Tomia didn't feel natural, but at the same time, the female felt like she was nature itself. The drink of water was helping, but Imra was still struggling to discern exactly who or what Tomia was. Imra acquiesced. It did not matter who she was getting her help from or why. She would be at Millspare soon. She would figure out the rest once she arrived.

Imra got to her feet and turned to hand the water skin back to Tomia. Tomia, and the rock she had been sitting on, were gone.

"Thank you, Tomia," Imra said into the gentle breeze around her.

It was time to move. Imra climbed to her feet, pulling the strap of the water skin over her head. She didn't feel the subtle but familiar pull inside of her to help determine the direction she should walk. *Well, that's good news, I suppose. It means there is no threat to my life right now. I always wondered what that would feel like.*

Though elated at the prospect of safety, the seeress was disheartened that her power might prove useless in Lillerem. Her magic guided her away from danger. In the past, this had been synonymous with guiding her to where she needed to be. Imra, with her power of premonition, and only miles from her destination, was lost. There was a pretty tree in the distance to her left, so Imra decided it looked like a good choice for a direction in which to travel.

Three steps into her walk, her travels were halted by a skunk. Imra was sure the animal had appeared in the milliseconds it had taken to blink. Pretty tree in the distance or not, the chance of being sprayed by the critter in her path made Imra change her mind about the direction she had picked. Imra changed course and was about to march off in the new direction when a brown bear stood on its hind legs just a few yards away. Exasperated, Imra picked another direction and started walking. No natural threats blocked her path this time.

"Thank you, Tomia," Imra grumbled under her breath.

Tobias gave Daisy a scratch behind the ears. The houndsman was not a fool. He was caught. It was only a matter of time. Tobias had released the other kennel dogs before exiting Fallholm. Selfishly, he kept Daisy leashed beside him. She was a wonderful dog, and a small part of Tobias had hoped she would have been a companion for him if he had made it through the forest.

The hundespor had picked up Tobias's scent over an hour ago. They were in no rush, or he would be dead already. If Tobias did not release Daisy now, she would die with him. He kneeled down in front of the dog and looked into her sad eyes. Stroking the dog's head, Tobias accepted that he would not get to know what freedom felt like. From his pocket, Tobias pulled the small towel Alek always used to dry his hands after washing away the slop he fed to Skilanis's pets. He offered the towel up to Daisy to smell, which she did, and then he dropped the towel to the floor.

"Go get him, girl," he whispered to the dog.

Daisy sprinted off after her new quarry. Tobias sat on the ground next to Alek's towel and placed Daisy's leash in his lap. He rested his head on his knees to wait for death and think about the long life he had endured. For a slave, he had enjoyed life. Working with Ulford's hounds in the kennels had provided him with the companionship of the dogs, and he was able to avoid the strenuous work of the fields. Tobias did not regret what he had done to earn his station of relative comfort. Tobias was glad Alek had never bothered to ask how he got his place working in the kennels. At least the boy would remember Tobias fondly.

The sound of crunching leaves came from the left, then there was crunching on the right. In moments, the hundespor stood in a loose circle around Tobias. He did not look up. He waited for them to strike and hoped the pain of the initial bites would be over quickly and put an end to the waiting. The first bite never came. Instead, a male voice met Tobias's ears.

"Houndsman, it's been some time since we've spoken. I must say, I was not expecting to find you here alone."

"It has been a while, Captain Bakken. Please, call me Tobias. We are still family, after all."

The relatively pleasant smile Bakken was wearing disappeared with Tobias's suggestion that he was family. The captain grabbed the older elf by the shirt collar and dragged him to his feet. He pushed Tobias up against a nearby tree and leaned in close.

"Do not pretend we are blood," Bakken snarled. "She was my sister, and you promised before the gods to protect her for eternity. You did quite the opposite. I have been waiting for an excuse to cause you pain for a long time."

"I see you still have not accepted that my actions were not of my volition," sighed Tobias. "As I once explained, she was ill. It was at her request that I ended her life. I loved her. My love for her was so strong, I condemned my soul to Helheim for her. I became a murderer for her."

"She could have lived. She could have fought it. You didn't even try to help her," said Bakken.

"I fear we have had this circular conversation before. It might be best if we skip to the reason for the hundespor hunt this evening," said Tobias.

Bakken did not have the opportunity to reply. A voice like the hiss of a snake came from a figure that appeared to glide into the clearing from among the trees.

"What did you do with the boy?"

Tobias watched the Master approach. Tobias couldn't speak. He had expected Skilanis to send the hundespor after him. Captain Bakken's presence wasn't even that surprising. His brother-in-law had likely jumped at the chance to aid in the hunt, but Tobias could not fathom why Skilanis would come himself. Tobias replayed the question Skilanis had asked. He was not a smart elf, but he understood it after a few moments of thought. Skilanis did not want Tobias dead. That was not the goal. Skilanis wanted information about Alek.

Tobias needed to make a choice. He could tell Skilanis that the boy had not been with him. Tobias had been unconscious when Alek left, but he knew Alek had disappeared at the same time the princess was rescued from her cage. There was a chance Alek was with her. Tobias could give Skilanis this information in exchange for his life. He should try. This was how a slave lived to be as old as Tobias. If the boy was with the princess, he was well protected. The Master would figure it out eventually, anyway.

The other option was to lead Skilanis in the wrong direction. Tobias could tell the Slave Master that he and Alek had hoped to reach Gulentine Palace and ask for help with freeing the slaves of Dredfall. Tobias could suggest that Alek had gone ahead because he was faster on his own. This would send Skilanis in the opposite direction from the castle where Kindra and Alek were likely to be.

It didn't matter which option Tobias selected. Skilanis was not going to allow Tobias to live out the rest of his days as a free person. Either Tobias would die here in the Dredskog, or he would die back in Fallholm as a slave. The choice Tobias made would only make a difference for Alek and the future the boy might secure in Lillerem.

CHAPTER 12

Butch and Cassidy both got to their feet at the same time. Jess had been about to pull off her clothes and get ready for bed when the German Shepherd dogs went to the small window of the bedchamber. Jess moved to stand behind them. The dogs had their paws up on the windowsill, and their fluffy bodies blocked Jess's view of the courtyard below. Jess looked inside her mind and viewed the world through the eyes of the dogs instead.

After adjusting to using vision that was primarily shades of gray, Jess scanned the ground. Butch and Cassidy were both focused on the smell that had drawn them to the window, and they were trying to spot the source of the fragrance. Instinctively, Jess recognized the scent as that of another dog. It was not unheard of for there to be dogs in Alfheim, though it was much rarer than in the human realm. People in Alfheim did not keep dogs as pets. Dogs were used primarily by hunters or those who kept livestock. The lone dog prowling somewhere below was unusual.

A howl came from below. It wasn't like the howl of a wolf. It was more like the bay of a hound. Butch and Cassidy slammed their front paws onto the floor and ran to the door. The move was eerily similar to the way they acted when the mail was delivered or there was a squirrel in the yard back home. Jess smiled. Her dogs were just being dogs. There was no actual threat. She sent the dogs some soothing thoughts and sat on the bed to remove her boots. Jess only had one boot off when an unmistakable voice came from below. Jess pulled her boot back on and headed for the courtyard.

"Alek! I said to wait for me! Where are we going?" asked Riva.

"There is no 'we'. I didn't say you could come too," grumbled Alek.

"It's a little hard not to notice you leaving when we were sleeping in the same room," replied Riva. "I wanted to know why you were sneaking off."

"You were sleeping, I wasn't. You're the one who said I should share your room until Mildred gives me one of my own. If you let me stay with Einar and Mildred, then you wouldn't be awake and you wouldn't be out here," Alek argued.

Riva laughed. "You have no idea. If you stayed with Einar and Mildred, you wouldn't be out here, either. Mildred is like a hawk. You wouldn't have been able to get within a step of the door without her ordering you back to bed."

Alek squatted down near a bush. "Is that you, girl?"

Riva let out a squeal of pleasure when a black-and-tan hound emerged from the shadows. The dog went straight to Alek and started licking his face and hands.

Alek turned to Riva and gave her a hard look. Riva clamped her hand over her own mouth but couldn't hide her excitement.

"Ok, come here and meet her," Alek said. "This is Daisy. She's one of Ulford's hounds. I have no idea how she found me, but she's a good girl."

"She's probably starving," said Riva. "Let's bring her inside. We can steal some of Butch and Cassidy's food for her."

"You'll do what?" asked a voice from the direction the two young elves had come.

Slowly, Riva and Alek turned. They remained squatting as they spun in place, keeping Daisy shielded behind them. There was always a chance the dog wouldn't be noticed. The Elven children looked up at Jess from their spot near the ground. Alek was desperately trying to think of an excuse for the nighttime excursion into the courtyard when Butch and Cassidy stepped up on either side of Jess. There was no way Daisy was going to go unnoticed now.

Panic closed in on Alek's heart as he watched Butch's hackles rise. The Shepherd was preparing to tear poor Daisy apart. Alek chanced a quick look at Riva and saw her face was full of alarm. Daisy, never being a dog to understand danger, chose that moment to pop her head between Alek and Riva. She tilted her head at Butch with interest. Butch took a step forward and lowered his head slightly. Alek could see the German Shepherd's teeth clearly. He felt it then. It was confusing at first, but Alek was sure he felt amusement emanating from Jess. Alek looked into Jess's eyes and took in her harsh, reprimanding gaze. It made him want to curl up inside himself. He closed his eyes and felt her emotions instead of trying to read them from her expression. *Jess is trying not to laugh.*

Alek stood, keeping his hand on Daisy's neck so he could grab her if she ran. He did his best to ignore Butch's snarling presence and met Jess's gaze instead. Riva stood as well, but she did not look as confident as Alek was managing to appear. Riva looked like she was seconds from running back inside.

At last, Jess cracked a smile. "You are either incredibly brave, or you really like that hound."

Alek was not about to share that he had been aware of Jess's feelings before she had smiled and revealed her intentions to him. As soon as Jess smiled, Butch relaxed as well. He did not back up, but his hackles lowered and his teeth were no longer on display. Alek stepped a little farther from Riva to allow Daisy to emerge through the gap. Cassidy stood from where he had been sitting beside Jess and came forward to give Daisy a sniff. He must have approved because he returned to Jess's side and plopped down onto the ground, bored.

"This is Daisy," Alek introduced the hound to Jess.

"I heard," replied Jess. "She is one of Ulford's hounds. Do you know why she would have followed you here?"

Alek stepped a little closer to the black-and-tan hound. He ran his hands over her head and down one of her long ears protectively. He had no idea why the dog was here or how she had found him. There was the possibility Ulford had sent Tobias and the hounds to hunt Alek down, and even if that was the case, he did not think the dogs would have traveled this far alone. There was no sign of any other hounds, or of Tobias, so Alek found he was as ignorant as Jess.

"I don't know why she is here, and I don't know how she got this far alone. I know she won't hurt us though," Alek said.

Jess squatted down in front of the young elves. She reached out her hands as if beckoning Daisy forward. At first, Daisy pulled back slightly, and then she took a few steps forward and sniffed Jess's hands. Deciding she was safe with Jess, Daisy pushed herself closer until she nearly knocked Jess onto her rear. Jess put her arms around the dog and rubbed her, making soothing sounds until Cassidy stuck his nose under Jess's arm to let his mother know he was getting jealous. When Jess pulled away from the hound, she looked unsettled.

"I think we should all go inside," said Jess. "You have my permission to take some dog food for Daisy. There are extra bowls in the kitchen. Grab one to fill with water as well. Daisy can sleep with the two of you tonight."

Jess walked ahead of the younger elves. Butch walked on her left, and Cassidy took up the space on Jess's right. Alek understood that Jess was not angry with him, but something was still off. He stretched himself out to her to take in her feelings. He was surprised to find urgency and fear. Jess looked relaxed, and as in control of the situation as ever, but Alek could feel her panic rising. For now, he was happy to return to Riva's room with Daisy, but he knew something was the matter.

As soon as they were inside, Jess gave an almost imperceptible nod, and Butch and Cassidy dispersed in opposite directions. Riva ran off to grab food and water for Daisy. Jess pointed down the hall to the castle wing comprised almost entirely of Riva's rooms. Alek gave a quick whistle and Daisy followed him down the hall. They only waited a few moments before Riva returned and closed the door behind her.

"Something is wrong," Alek said immediately. "I don't know why, but after Jess saw Daisy, she was scared."

"I doubt it was what Jess saw that scared her," Riva said as she placed the bowls of food and water on the floor.

"It had to be. I knew she was kidding when she was acting all mad, but after she met Daisy, she was scared."

"It wasn't what she *saw* that scared her," repeated Riva. "It was probably whatever Daisy told her."

"What? Daisy can't talk," Alek said incredulously. He gestured to the hound that was voraciously consuming her food.

"All animals can talk to Jess if they want to, and Jess can talk back to them. Well, I guess it's not really talking, but they can speak through pictures. They like, they kinda see each other's memories and thoughts," said Riva. "That reminds me. How did you know Jess wasn't really mad? She had her teacher-face on and everything!"

"Can I trust you?" Alek asked.

"Of course," answered Riva.

Alek was not comforted by the speed and ease with which Riva had answered. He really wasn't even sure what there was to tell. It was only tonight that the thoughts had started to make sense to him. He was not sure how he would begin to try to explain it to someone else. It was too late to change his mind. Riva was waiting, expectantly, for a secret. Alek went with one that was more embarrassing, but less likely to scare Riva off.

"I don't know how to read," Alek admitted.

"I kinda figured." Riva laughed involuntarily as she replied.

Alek was mortified. He searched his memories for something he might have said or done to tip Riva off about his secret. If the girl had been perceptive enough to uncover his inability to read, it might be possible that she also knew he could read people's feelings. The look on Alek's face caused Riva to soften when she spoke next.

"I'm sorry. The laugh wasn't because you can't read. I laughed because I found it funny that you thought anyone would expect you could. Relax, there isn't a soul that would hold not being able to read against you, anyway. Until last night, you were a slave. It's not like slave owners go around teaching their slaves written communication. That would only make it easier for a bunch of people to plan an escape!"

Alek was not sure how he felt about Riva's explanation. On one hand, he was affronted that she had assumed he couldn't read, but on the other hand, she had been correct. Logically, it made sense for a slave owner to prevent people from reading, not to encourage it.

"Anyway," said Riva. "That wasn't your real secret. Tell me your truth."

Alek said nothing for a moment. He was, again, forced to acknowledge how perceptive Riva was. It was already impossible to keep secrets from this elf, so he decided it was better to come clean. If Alek didn't confide in Riva, she would feel as if he did not trust her. Alek didn't want that. He really wanted a friend and trust was important between friends.

"I think I have a power," Alek confided to Riva.

Riva let out a little laugh. "You think you do, or you know you do? There's a difference."

"I only started to notice it tonight, so I'm really not sure. I was sitting around the table at supper with everyone and I was able to feel what each person was feeling inside. The thing that made me notice is that what the people felt wasn't what was on their faces. Like… I felt like I knew their insides better than their outsides," said Alek.

"That sounds gross," said Riva.

"It's not a joke, Riva. No one else I knew in Dredfall had powers. I was always able to move things around with my mind, but this thing with the feelings is new."

Riva met Alek's gaze and became more serious. "How many people did you really spend time with while you were in Dredfall?"

"I played football with the other kids all the time. There was also Tobias in the kennels and then Kindra was there, too. I was with her almost all day long," replied Alek.

"Ok," said Riva. "How did Kindra feel about being locked up? What was Tobias feeling?"

"Well, both of them were always kinda sad. That doesn't count, though. I would've known they were sad even if I didn't feel it."

"Let's try again," said Riva. "How did the other kids feel?"

"I'm starting to see your point," said Alek. "I'm not sure I've ever been in a situation where someone was hiding their real feelings. If the feelings on the outside match the feelings on the inside, I wouldn't have realized I could read feelings."

"You're not as hopeless as I thought," Riva said.

"Anyway," said Alek, "I just told you I can tell what people are feeling. Why doesn't it bother you that I have powers? Is it because you're used to Jess's powers already?"

The room grew ice cold in seconds. Alek exhaled and watched his breath turn to smoke in front of his face. Before he could back away from Riva, his feet were covered in a thin layer of ice and he was immobilized. Then, with Riva giggling the entire time, it began to snow.

Alek and Riva were late getting down to the kitchen the next morning. Riva had let the snow accumulate to almost a half an inch before deciding she had made her point. She and Alek had spent thirty minutes using towels to soak up water from the floor after the room warmed up. Once the floor was dry, Riva had offered to teach Alek his letters. The two elves had stayed up long enough for Alek to learn to write his own name flawlessly.

The children had slept late. Alek, with no wardrobe or room of his own yet, had slept in his clothes from the day before and was still wearing them. He had taken Daisy for a walk while Riva cleaned herself up and got dressed, and then returned to her rooms to wash his face and hands in an attempt to look presentable.

The young elves entered the kitchen to find only Kindra and Jess at the table. Einar motioned from the stove for Alek and Riva to sit as well. The red-faced older elf hobbled over with two bowls of oatmeal and placed them on the table. Alek remembered to say thank you, but only after hearing Riva say it and then seeing the glare she directed his way.

"You should practice that one with care," Jess said. "If you can't master 'please' and 'thank you', Mildred will have you and Daisy living out in the stable."

"Aunt Jess, Aunt Kindra, guess what!" said Riva. "Alek has powers!"

Alek's stomach dropped. He had sworn Riva to secrecy and really expected the girl to hold her tongue. The last thing he wanted was for everyone to start avoiding him because they were afraid he would be reading their emotions.

"Really?" asked Kindra. "Is he more powerful than you?"

"He can't control weather or anything, but his powers are pretty cool," said Riva.

Alek stared at Riva. Alek was learning fast. It felt good to have friends until they betrayed you.

"Alek can move things with his mind!" Riva said as if it were the most exciting news in the realms.

Alek released the breath he had been holding. Riva was laughing. Warmth radiated from her core as Alek realized the girl had been teasing him. *Seriously? She almost just stopped my heart!*

"Prove it," Jess was saying.

Alek promptly commanded the oatmeal on Riva's spoon to hop onto her nose. Riva's mouth fell open, and she went completely still. A clump of the oatmeal fell into her gaping maw. It was Alek's turn to giggle. Jess and Kindra looked at each other and rolled their eyes.

"I do not envy Mildred if there are going to be two of them running around Millspare," said Kindra.

The rest of the oatmeal from Riva's nose fell toward her lap, but her clothing was rescued. Daisy moved like lightning to grab the clump from mid-air.

"Great," said Kindra. "Even the dog lacks table manners. Mildred is going to go to an early grave."

The room went completely silent as a slim blonde entered the room through the servants' door without making a sound. Imra stood in the doorway, kneading her hands as if she were unsure what to do with them. Time was only frozen for a moment before the people in the room took action.

Jess and Kindra sprang to their feet. Kindra raised a hand and Imra flew back out through the doorway she had recently occupied. Butch and Cassidy sprinted down the hall after Syndral's twin, with Jess and Kindra following at a more leisurely pace.

"Maybe we should go upstairs?" Riva asked.

"Why?" asked Alek. "No one told us we had to leave. If we find a place to sit still and we're quiet, maybe we'll get to find out what's going on for once."

"Do you know who that lady was? She looks almost exactly like my mom."

Alek nodded. "That's Imra. She's Ulford's mistress. I don't know what made her think she could walk into this castle without dying, but I suspect Butch and Cassidy will be the first to point out her mistake."

CHAPTER 13

Leif's chin hit the back of his horse's neck, causing him to bite his tongue. It only bled for a moment before his magic healed the wound. Leif had taken an extra dose of Trego's mushroom tincture this morning. The concoction had been doing an excellent job of keeping Leif from experiencing the cycles of anxiety and depression that would have otherwise sent him running back to the human realm where he could self-medicate.

The existence of Trego's brew was the only reason Leif had agreed to remain after Joral and Gunnar had kidnapped him from his cabin and brought him to Alfheim to help rescue Kindra. Leif's ability to steal a little extra of the mixture on a regular basis so he could enjoy its effects recreationally was the reason Leif was still in Alfheim, even though Kindra was no longer a captive.

Now, riding into the Dredskog and unable to keep his eyes open, Leif had to admit to himself he may have taken too much of the tincture before heading out on this journey. The trip was unexpected. Leif had stumbled into the kitchen, feeling as if his head were floating and not having a care in the world, just in time to hear Jess explaining what she had seen in Daisy's mind. Leif, Joral, Gunnar, Bane and Krish were now on a mission to find Daisy's caretaker. The houndsman from Ulford's kennel was probably dead already, but it was possible he had survived the night.

"You alright brother?" Gunnar asked Leif.

Leif, clearly not alright, threw Gunnar a lazy thumbs up. Gunnar rolled his eyes. If it were anyone other than Leif, Gunnar would have sent the elf back to the castle as soon as he started nodding off on his horse. Gunnar had not only witnessed his brother fight under the influence of many substances, but had personally fought him when Leif was in less than top form. Leif was nearly unbeatable, even when he was not sober.

Gunnar switched his thoughts to the task ahead. They needed to find Tobias. If he was still alive, the houndsman might have valuable information about Skilanis. The princes could also offer him an escort through the forest and into Lillerem to begin life as someone other than a slave. The likelihood that Tobias was alive was small. Jess had said Daisy's last moments with Tobias played out more like a 'goodbye' than a call to be rescued. Tobias had sent Daisy to find Alek, not to find help. Gunnar was able to admit his newly discovered son was not the kind of help Tobias would have needed to get through the Dredskog.

Picking carefully through the forest on horseback, Gunnar found himself falling behind Krish, Joral, and Bane as he tried to ensure his reckless brother didn't fall from his horse. The rest of the group was no longer within earshot and Gunnar contemplated suggesting that Leif stay behind while Gunnar rode to catch up.

"Listen, I don't know how much of Trego's potion you drank this morning, but I feel like you are more of a hindrance than a help right now. Maybe it would be better if you turned that horse around and headed back?"

"And miss out on all this fun? Besides, we're bonding! You don't need to worry about me. I feel great!" Leif replied.

"I'm sure you do, brother. You certainly look as if you are feeling wonderful, but it is not you I'm concerned for."

"Gunnar! Leif!" Joral called loudly from somewhere up ahead.

Gunnar kicked his horse and took off in the direction of the sound. He could hear Leif's horse right behind him. The brothers rode into a clearing and were met by a gruesome scene. An older elf hung from a large tree. There was no rope. The male's body was suspended by several large metal spikes through his shoulders and torso. Joral was standing within inches of the tree with his head turned, as if listening to something. Gunnar swallowed hard. The old elf was still alive.

Bane let out a roar and fell onto his back. A hundespor pinned him to the ground. Krish stepped forward and separated the creature's head from its body with a slice of his sword. Before Bane could regain his feet, more hundespor entered the clearing. The princes were surrounded. Joral and Gunnar fought back to back, each keeping several hundespor at bay. Bane gained his feet and grabbed the tail of one of the creatures. Bane's massive body lifted the dog-like creature into the air and hurled it toward several others. Three of the creatures rolled to the ground, including the one Bane had used as a projectile. Krish ran his sword through each of them.

A hundespor swiped at Joral's legs and the prince hit the ground hard. Gunnar felt Joral go down behind him, but was unable to take his eyes from the two hundespor he was currently battling. Bane and Krish were on the other side of the clearing. Joral screamed in pain, and Gunnar feared Joral would be lost. Leif, still on horseback, rode by and threw a hand down to Joral. Joral pulled up and seated himself behind Leif. Blood flowed from Joral's calf where a hundespor had clawed him open.

Leif dropped Joral at the edge of the clearing so the elf could take care of his leg wound. Leif charged back toward the fight. He nearly tumbled to the ground on his first drive, but managed to regain his balance before he lost his saddle. Leif's sword had only grazed the back of the hundespor he had lunged toward. He turned his horse and settled his gaze on two hundespor facing him. The two creatures merged into one, then split back into two blurry beasts again. Leif squeezed his eyes tight, trying to force them to focus, then charged the moment he reopened them. This time, his blade struck true when he charged, but driving back and forth was making him dizzy.

Gunnar ran his sword through the skull of the final hundespor he had been battling and he spun to aid Bane and Krish. Krish went down on his face as giant paws slammed into his back. Gunnar charged toward the Crown Prince, but he was too far away. Leif spun his horse toward Krish and extended his arm. A flash of bright light erupted from Leif's palm and Gunnar threw his hands up to shield his eyes. The sound of trees splintering and crashing to the ground assaulted Gunnar as he was hit on the head by a large branch that turned his vision to black.

Gunnar's ears were ringing. He listened for the snarls of the hundespor, but only heard Joral yelling Krish's name. Joral yelled again and again. Gunnar managed to push a huge branch off of himself and get to his hands and knees. His vision was blurry, but he could see Bane tearing the body of a hundespor off of Krish. Joral, already hurrying toward the Crown Prince, slid to the ground beside Krish, dislodging the bandage he had only recently secured to his leg. Joral grabbed Krish's shoulders and pulled him up enough for Gunnar to see a gaping hole in the Crown Prince's chest.

Gunnar's head was throbbing, but he could feel his body working to mend itself. He dragged himself to his feet and the pain at the base of his skull started to ebb, at last. His vision was clear by the time he reached Krish's side. Joral was no longer yelling Krish's name. He remained on his knees next to the body of the Crown Prince of Lillerem. Slowly, Gunnar turned his head to look at Leif.

"What have you done, brother?" Gunnar growled.

Leif did not answer. He slid from his horse and hit the ground with a soft thud. Either Leif was not using his magic to control his descent, or he was having difficulty wielding his powers. Leif moved slowly toward Krish's body. He stumbled and nearly fell, but managed to propel himself to a place among the gathered princes before the ground claimed him. Leif's knees hit hard enough to make the others wince, but Leif did not feel any pain. He could not take his eyes from the hole in Krish's chest.

Waves of emotion crashed down on Leif as he took in the destruction he had brought on with his magical strike. The bloody pit in the Crown Prince's chest was not the result of a hundespor tearing flesh. That hole was nearly circular; a puncture directly through the heart. Leif had used a magical lightning strike, but his aim had been unsteady. Instead of striking the hundespor that had Krish pinned to the ground, the strike had brought down a tree. A large branch had speared the hundespor and killed it. The death of the hundespor should have saved Krish's life, but the branch that killed the beast had continued through its flesh and entered the chest of the Crown Prince.

"It's not your fault, Leif," Joral was quick to say. "You were trying to use the tree to kill the hundespor. You couldn't know this was going to happen."

"I wasn't aiming for the trees," whispered Leif.

Leif whirled to face Gunnar. "You knew! You knew I shouldn't be here. Why didn't you stop me? Why didn't you send me back to Millspare?"

Gunnar turned his gaze from Krish's body to stare down his brother. He set his jaw and started moving toward Leif. Joral jumped between the two elves, facing Gunnar and trying to slow his progress.

"Gunnar, you know this is how he is. He doesn't mean it. It always takes him time to accept responsibility. He knows this isn't your fault," said Joral.

Gunnar stopped walking toward Leif and turned his focus toward Joral. "You're right! That's how it always is! Leif screws up and instead of blaming him for his incompetence, we make excuses for him! Which illness would you like to use as his defense this time? Is it because he's an addict? Is it the depression or the anxiety that caused this? It is our fault, Joral! We are the ones who brought him back to Alfheim. We wanted his power badly enough to risk his ineptitude. We were the ones that had Trego find a substance that would keep Leif happily ignorant of reality. It was our selfishness that had us believing it was an acceptable way to keep him from crawling back to his cycle of self-depreciation and oblivion in the human realm."

Gunnar sat down in the dirt and hung his head in defeat. Joral sat down on the ground next to Gunnar. He slowly re-wrapped his leg to give his hands something to do. Krish's blood, covering Joral's hands, bloodied the cloth further. Bane began wrapping the Crown Prince's body in a cloak of deep purple, the color representative of Gulentine Palace. Krish's body would need to be presented to King Erik, and the people of Lillerem would then be notified of the death of the heir to the throne. There was silence as Bane placed Krish's wrapped body across his horse. Bane mounted his mare and took hold of the reins from Krish's horse as well. Bane nodded to Joral and Gunnar and began the journey to Lillerem City.

"I'm glad I'm not him," Gunnar said.

"He's the best person for the task. He probably won't even say anything to the king. He'll just drop the horse with Krish's body off and leave it to the king's advisors to figure things out," Joral said. "Maybe I could learn something from Bane. If I spoke less often, people would just come to expect silence from me and I could keep to myself."

"It works for Bane, but that's not who you are," replied Gunnar. "They're probably going to imprison him."

"Bane? Why?" Joral was confused.

"No," Gunnar sighed. "My brother. The elf that just killed the Crown Prince of Lillerem. The person who just murdered his daughter's betrothed. It'll be interesting when we all get back to Millspare."

"I think it will just be the two of us returning," Joral said.

Gunnar looked up. Leif was no longer in the clearing.

"Maybe he went to Millspare to tell Kindra what happened?" Joral asked.

"This is Leif," replied Gunnar. "If you want to find him, he'll be at his cabin in the human realm, drowning himself in alcohol. With luck, he'll light a match and ignite the fumes wafting from his skin."

"You don't mean that," said Joral.

"I'm not so sure anymore," replied Gunnar. "This has been my entire life. I raised Leif from a toddler in the human realm. I was responsible for him and his actions for over a hundred years while he matured." Gunnar huffed out a laugh. "Matured may be the incorrect word. Once Leif appeared to be of an adult age in the human realm, I came back to Alfheim to join my family. I left Leif to destroy his own life however he desired. All that changed when Kindra dug him out of a whiskey barrel and he followed her here to Alfheim. Now, I feel like we are children again. I feel like he is still my responsibility."

Gunnar nodded toward the tree where the body of the houndsman still hung. "We should pull him down and bring him out of the forest. We can burn him in the fields of Lillerem so his soul can roam free."

Joral nodded and stood. Gunnar grabbed Joral's hand to stop him.

"What did Tobias say before the attack? I saw you listening closely as life left Tobias's eyes."

"With all this going on, I pushed that aside." Joral gestured to the bodies of the hundespor littering the clearing. "Tobias told me to protect the boy. Skilanis is after Alek."

Gunnar paled. Thoughts of Leif instantaneously seemed inconsequential. If there was a single person Gunnar absolutely knew he was responsible for, it was Alek. Gunnar had not been able to protect his son for the boy's early years, but he would dedicate the rest of his life to sheltering Alek from harm.

"Why would Skilanis be after Alek?" asked Gunnar.

"I do not know. I'm not even sure Tobias knew the answer to that question. The old houndsman had little breath to share words when we arrived," replied Joral.

"Humor me for a moment," said Gunar. "What could Skilanis expect from the boy?"

"I truly have no answer, and it matters little anyhow. It isn't possible for a logical person to predict what that mad elf intends to do from one moment to the next. The only thing we can safely assume is that Skilanis's plans will not have a positive outcome for Alek. I'm glad he is under our protection."

"You make a good point, my friend," replied Gunnar. "We will continue to keep the boy safe, regardless. Now, we should start back to Millspare. We need to inform Kindra and the others of Krish's death. I hate that we are about to turn her world upside down."

CHAPTER 14

Imra sat with her back to the corner of the kitchen table. She sat sideways in her chair with her feet pointed toward the door as if hoping she might be able to run from the room, but Butch and Cassidy assured her compliance and immobility. Syndral paced in front of Imra, trying to gain control of her rage. Kindra leaned against the far end of the table, waiting for Syndral to relax enough to begin asking questions. Jess sat beside her friend, feeling more anxious with every second she watched Syndral pace. Alek and Riva had retreated back into the area where Einar prepared the food. They had a clear view of the action at the table, but they were removed enough that no one was taking notice of their presence.

"Let's start over," Syndral said. "How did Ulford die if you knew the princes were coming to kill him?"

"I told you," replied Imra. "The only explanation is that I would have died if Ulford had survived the attack on the training grounds. That's the way my magic works. It shows me the best path to achieve my goals except when my goal will put my life in danger. Above all other things, my magic guides me on the path that keeps me alive. Since my goal has always been to help Ulford take Lillerem, and I didn't foresee a way to avoid his death, it means I would have died if I had tried to save Ulford from Skilanis. I don't know why you're the one who is so upset, anyway. You're the one who went and switched sides. If anything, I should be angry with you!"

Imra was yelling now, but the fire in Syndral's eyes showed she was not going to be outdone.

"You are my sister and I trusted you! You told me you would keep Ulford's attention away from Riva!"

Imra stood to meet Syndral's glare. "I did what you asked. Riva was safe in the human realm for over forty years. You were the one who decided to go find her and forgot to return to Castle Bindrell when your leave was up. You aligned with the enemy!"

"Maybe I wouldn't have needed to go elsewhere for help if you had kept that psychopath, Skilanis, from sending out his pets. They found her, Imra!"

"You should have trusted me. I never would have let him hurt Riva!"

"You did a fine job protecting Ulford from death by his own assassin! I trust Lillerem royalty over your self-preservation any day of the week," Syndral seethed.

"Trust?" The smile on Imra's lips was not one of kindness. "You trust them? Do you trust them to the point where you have even bothered to tell them who Riva's father is? They might be too polite to ask, but they must be wondering. You wield a great deal of healing strength, Syndral, but you have no other magical power. Your new friends must be curious to know how Riva ended up with such an incredible gift."

As if she suddenly felt their presence, Syndral spun toward the young elves eavesdropping on the other side of the kitchen. Alek ducked, but he was slow in pulling Riva down with him. Syndral put her index finger up in her sister's direction to keep her from speaking.

"Riva? You need to come out here, now," Syndral called to her daughter.

Alek gave the girl a little shove. Riva stumbled into view and started walking toward her mother.

"You too, Alek. Come over here."

Alek stepped out from behind the large cooktop he and Riva had used as cover. He pushed his floppy hair out of his eyes, but it immediately fell back into his face. He and Riva stood before Syndral with their eyes lowered.

"Neither of you has done anything wrong," said Syndral. "I am going to continue this conversation with my sister. Kindra and Jess are going to make sure the two of you go back to Riva's room."

Kindra and Jess turned their heads toward Syndral, wearing similar looks of disbelief. Neither of them wanted to leave Imra and Syndral alone in Castle Millspare. Jess was concerned that one or both of them might pose a threat to the castle's occupants, but Kindra simply didn't want to miss the best part of the conversation. Syndral felt the inevitable protest building within the two friends and spoke before they could challenge her directive.

"I know you have an interest in keeping those within Millspare safe. Jess, you might want to consider leaving your canine weapons with me."

Jess instantly understood the concession Syndral was making. She ushered the children and her best friend out of the kitchen immediately. She hurried the group down the hall, urging them to move quickly.

"What the hell, Jess? We're going to miss out on all the secrets," Kindra protested.

"That's exactly what is going to happen if we don't get somewhere quiet, so I can concentrate," replied Jess.

"Oh! I get it," Riva said. "Aunt Jess wants to use Butch and Cassidy's eyes!"

"She is a smart one, isn't she?" Kindra murmured.

Alek, Riva and Kindra spilled into Riva's chambers. Daisy looked up from the spot she had commandeered on Riva's bed. The door swung shut and Alek heard something slide down the length of the opposite side. Jess had not entered the room. She had plopped herself down in the hall just outside. Alek accepted that. It wasn't like Jess was going to sit there and give them a play-by-play of the conversation in the kitchen. He wasn't sure he would have been able to sit around, silently waiting for a report either, so it was a good thing Jess was in the hall where she wouldn't be disturbed.

Alek sat on the bed next to Daisy and started petting the hound. Riva joined him and Daisy rolled over to offer the Elven children her belly. The dog had adapted to palace life quickly. Since arriving in the night, she had already learned to travel between Riva's bedroom and the kitchen to alternate between her two favorite activities; eating and sleeping.

Kindra was the one pacing now. Patience was not one of her stronger qualities.

"Hey, Riva," said Alek. "You don't know who your father is, do you?"

"Nope," Riva answered. "I asked my mother, but she told me it didn't matter. Honestly, I was still so shocked to know my birth mother that I never pressed her for the birth-father information."

"I get that," said Alek. "I learnt who both my parents are all at once. It was pretty intense that way. I think it's better to find those things out a little at a time."

Kindra cut into the conversation. "*Nope. Learnt.* Mildred would be in such pain right now if she were in this room listening to the words you two are using."

"Forgive us, O educated one," Riva said as she rolled her eyes.

"Sometimes I forget we brought you to Alfheim just when you were mastering the role of a teenage human girl," Kindra said under her breath.

"Speaking as an ex-prison guard, the secret to passing time is to keep busy. Engaging in conversation helps," Alek said to Kindra.

Kindra stopped pacing. She went over and pulled the high-backed wooden chair from where it was pushed in beneath Riva's desk. Kindra placed the chair near the bed and sat down. She stared at the children for a moment before speaking.

"Imra made a good point. A power like yours must come from a strong line, Riva. Elves like your mother and Gunnar descend from King Andril. That is the most powerful magical line in the Kingdom of Lillerem, and they still don't have power like yours.

"I thought for sure your father was Pakk, but he died several years before you were born. Now that I know Syndral better, I can't see her having been in the bed of any male from Lillerem, anyway," Kindra mused.

"I bet Riva's dad was a bad guy. That's probably why Riva's mom doesn't want anyone to know who he is," said Alek.

Riva was quiet. She stroked Daisy's ears and pointedly avoided joining the conversation. Kindra looked as if she were about to voice another thought on Riva's bloodline when Alek shook his head quickly. He felt the sadness and confusion from within Riva. His and Kindra's words were making her uncomfortable. Alek hadn't considered that Riva's love for speculation and drawing conclusions would not extend to her own life. Kindra had closed her mouth, but the pensive look she wore suggested she was continuing the conversation within her head. Alek was comfortable with that. All he wanted was to keep Riva from hurting. Since Riva couldn't read thoughts or emotions, Kindra could think about Riva's paternity all she desired.

Alek grabbed a pen and quill from Riva's desk. He needed to keep Kindra's thoughts in her head and distract Riva from the recent topic of conversation.

"Riva, could you teach me some more words?"

Riva smiled and glanced hesitantly in Kindra's direction.

"It's ok," Alek said. "It's not like I can hide it forever, and like you told me, no one expects a slave to be able to read, anyway."

Kindra did not seem to notice the lesson on reading and writing three-letter words as it commenced on Riva's bed. Kindra was sifting through a mental family tree of likely fathers for Riva. All three people in the room were finding success passing time.

Jess entered the room a short time later. She gave the children a look that told them they were expected to stay put and then curled her finger to beckon Kindra out into the hall. As soon as the door closed, Alek crossed the room and pressed his ear to the wood to hear what the friends were saying. Riva started to protest, but Alek held up his hand and listened intently. After a minute, he stood and walked back over to his place on the bed.

Quietly, Alek whispered, "Jess is still in the hall. Leif is here. He asked for Kindra to meet him in the office by the main entrance."

Riva's eyes went wide. "What could he have to tell her that he didn't want the others to hear as well? Did the other princes return too?"

"I don't know any of that. Leif knows Jess can listen through her dogs, so he won't let them near the office. Jess won't be able to hear the conversation in the office, either. We're going to have to wait for Kindra to tell us," replied Alek.

"Tell us?" Riva laughed. "Don't you mean we are going to have to make sure we are close enough to listen in when Kindra tells the others? Whatever this is about, it's not something anyone is going to tell us about."

Alek looked up to catch the roguish twinkle in Riva's eyes. His first impression of this young girl had been off. She was not a spoiled princess, living in a castle. Riva had more in common with Alek than he had realized. Riva had not been raised by her parents and had only recently found out that Syndral was her mother. Since she was raised in the human realm, Riva had only recently been able to start exploring her power. She loved dogs, and it seemed as if she also had a propensity for getting into a little mischief. If Alek were a little older, he might think that he was falling in love.

Riva hopped off the bed and grabbed Alek's hand. She tugged him toward the wall next to her bed. Riva pulled the desk away from the wall and Alek heard a soft click. Riva pulled Alek in close and the semi-circle of space on which they stood slowly revolved with the wall in front of them. When the entrance to the passage stopped moving, Riva, Alek, and the desk were in the dark. After a moment, there was a spark as Riva lit an oil lamp. The flame's soft glow revealed a narrow hallway.

"Don't tell anyone I know this is here," Riva said.

Alek pressed his lips together and made the universal zipper motion to show his mouth would remain closed. Satisfied, Riva turned and led the way through the dim hallway. The ground sloped downward slightly until it reached a set of stone, spiral stairs. Riva took the stairs a little faster than was comfortable for Alek, and he had to push himself to remain in the circle of light provided by Riva's lantern. At the bottom of the stairs, Riva started down another hall. She stopped before reaching the end and pressed her face close to the wall.

"Ok, Leif and Kindra are in the office," Riva whispered.

Alek stepped up next to her and saw a small hole in the wall where light spilled through from the room beyond. Alek put his eye up to the hole and was able to see the interior of most of a small war room referred to as the office. Though the hole in the passage wall was about the height of Alek's chin, he found himself looking down at Leif and Kindra in the office on the other side. Leif was sitting in a leather chair and Kindra was pacing in front of an enormous map. *Is Kindra crying?*

Alek pulled back to share his observation with Riva, but her finger was to her lips. She shook her head to emphasize that they should not be talking. Alek kept his mouth shut and watched as Riva leaned in closer. *Is she about to kiss me?* Riva leaned in until their lips were inches apart, but her head kept moving forward. She placed her lips next to Alek's ear and spoke so softly, Alek had to hold his breath to be sure he didn't miss any of Riva's words.

"The walls are very thin. I brought us here to listen. There is no need to even look through the hole."

Alek leaned against the wall to eavesdrop. Riva sat down before doing likewise. Alek pulled back and then sat down too. He had only been standing for seconds and his neck had already felt stiff. Riva had obviously done this before.

Leif said, "Kindra, I regret my foolish actions. I am to blame for your loss."

"Hold on!" Kindra said harshly. "I'm trying to wrap my head around this. I step into the office and the first thing you tell me is that you accidentally killed Krish while trying to save him from a hundespor. That leaves out a lot of details. I'm not seeing how this is your fault. Also, I'm not sure I understand what you mean by killing him. Is this a joke?"

"I suspect it might be better if you sit down, Kindra. I came to tell you Krish is gone and to take responsibility for his death. If not for me, you would not need to suffer the loss of another mate."

"Where is his body?" Kindra asked. "I want to see him."

"Bane left immediately to present Krish's body to King Erik for a burning ceremony. I wanted to be sure you heard the news before the entire kingdom started receiving missives announcing the death of the Crown Prince."

Alek slowly let out the breath he had been holding. Kindra's betrothed, the Crown Prince, was dead. Alek had liked Krish. He was polite and very proper. Krish had completely met Alek's expectations for what a prince of Lillerem should be. Alek tried to imagine how Kindra was feeling, but it was impossible. He barely knew Krish, and he certainly was not in love with him. Alek was pretty sure he had never loved anyone. The closest thing to love Alek had known in his life was the respect and protection Tobias had offered him. The houndsman had been a little like a father figure, but Alek wasn't even clear on what *that* type of relationship was supposed to feel like. He gave up trying to put himself in Kindra's shoes.

Kindra asked, "Why are you taking responsibility for this?"

Leif did not answer right away. After a deep breath, all he offered was, "It's... complicated."

"Wait a minute. I know what complicated means when it comes to you. How is this possible? We're in Alfheim. You couldn't have been drunk. Your body would have healed you and shielded you from the effects of alcohol, or any other toxin, for that matter."

"Trego found at least one toxin with euphoric effects that is immune to my magic. It comes from some kind of mushroom and he has been mixing it up into a tincture for me to take. It's how Gunnar convinced me to stay in Alfheim to help rescue you," Leif said.

Alek flinched when Kindra yelled her reply. "You had to be convinced to help save me? You didn't just come because your daughter was in trouble? What happened to you wanting to protect me? Wasn't that the whole reason you ended up back here in Alfheim months ago, when you discovered I had stumbled through the gate in Norway and into this realm?"

There was no response from Leif, but one of the two people in the room got up and started pacing. Alek decided it was Kindra when she started speaking again. Her voice was slightly strained.

"Please tell me you didn't stay here after I was rescued just so you could keep enjoying Trego's concoction."

There was still no response from Leif. The pacing stopped. Alek pictured Kindra staring her father down as he sat, head bowed, in the chair.

"I suppose your silence is answer enough. I need to go speak to Trego," Kindra said.

"Kindra, wait," Leif pleaded. "We should talk about Krish. You must be hurting."

"There is nothing to say. He's gone. I don't want to talk about it, especially with you."

The door to the office opened and then slammed shut. Riva tugged at Alek's arm to get him moving. When they reached the staircase, she took the steps two at a time.

"Kindra will go to Jess," Riva said. "We need to get back to the room in case they go inside!"

Alek picked up his pace. He reached the top of the stairs and followed the light, glowing around Riva, up the hall. He tucked in close to her and her desk just as the click sounded and the wall started to rotate along with the semi-circular section of the floor. Before the movement ceased, Alek and Riva sprang for the bed. Daisy looked as if she hadn't moved the entire time they had been gone. Having a bed to sleep on for the first time in your life has that effect on hunting dogs. Alek and Riva flung themselves down beside the hound. The passageway sealed shut, and the door to Riva's room swung open less than a second later.

Jess pulled Kindra into the room and shut the door.

"What's wrong? Tell me what happened!"

Kindra shook her head. "I don't think I can talk about it without—I just need to sit down for a minute."

Kindra took a seat in the chair she had occupied earlier. She glanced at Alek and Riva and smiled faintly.

"Boy, I know I was chastising you two earlier, but you followed Jess's command to the letter. It doesn't look like either of you moved a muscle. Even Daisy is in the same position."

Riva and Alek exchanged a glance, but both kept from giving away their secret. Riva scooted toward the edge of the bed, in preparation for the dismissal she knew was imminent. Kindra put out her hand to stop her.

"Listen. There is nothing secret about what is happening. I was young once too. I am well aware that the more we try to conceal from you, the less you will trust us and the harder you will work to find out what's going on. You both can stay. Neither of you has had a very sheltered life, and I need to remember that though you are children, you have each been alive a few more years than Jess or I."

Raised among slaves in a country where death was a daily occurrence, Alek was nonplussed. Riva, still getting used to not being a thirteen-year-old human child, couldn't hide the surprise on her face as she slid back to the middle of the bed. She began stroking Daisy again as she quietly waited for Kindra to relay the story she and Alek already knew.

Surprisingly, Kindra controlled her emotions until she had nearly reached the end of the tale. The sensation that finally broke through was not sadness or despair. It was anger that pulled Kindra from the state of shock that had kept her feelings in check. As Kindra explained about her father using Trego's tincture as a source of entertainment, Alek nearly shrank backward across the bed to escape the wrath pulsing from within Kindra. Riva was still, but not alarmed, so Alek guessed she saw Kindra's anger, but was unaware of how volatile the feeling had caused Kindra to become.

"Let's try a few deep breaths, Kindra," said Jess. "You have every right to be angry at Leif for taking the tincture, and you have the same right to be angry with Trego for supplying it in the first place."

"You left out my anger toward my friends for luring my father here with the promise of a mind-altering substance, as well as more anger toward my father for needing to be lured here at all," Kindra yelled back at Jess.

"You're right," said Jess calmly. "You should direct some of that anger at me as well. If anyone should have known that bringing Leif here against his will was a bad idea, it should have been me. Honestly, if I had put my foot down when Krish suggested it, we wouldn't be in this mess and your fiancé would still be alive."

"Oh, no you don't. I see what you're doing, Jess. You can't take on all the blame here. You just admitted that it was Krish's idea to force Leif into helping with my rescue."

"Regardless," said Jess, "I feel some responsibility for your loss."

Kindra visibly deflated. The anger Alek had felt pressing on him did not dissipate, it simply vanished and was replaced with a dull emptiness. Alek appreciated his new talent for feeling other people's emotions, but at this moment, he was wishing he could read thoughts instead. Emotions were unpredictable and often irrational. After the news of Krish's death, looking inside to absorb Kindra's feelings was akin to a riding an unbroken horse.

Alek directed his magic toward Jess. She was awash with sorrow and regret. Jess wore a mask of calm, but Alek felt that she was hurting as much as Kindra was. It was more than confusing for the young elf. Jess was not in love with Krish, so Alek could see no reason for her to be filled with so much sorrow. Jess took Kindra's hand and squeezed it gently. Alek felt love emanating from both women.

"I can't believe he's really gone," said Kindra. "I feel like there was so much we never even had the chance to learn about one another."

"I'm so sorry you have to experience this," Jess said comfortingly. "It feels unfair that this is all happening to you again."

"That's the thing," said Kindra. "It's different this time. I'm devastated that Krish is dead. I'm angry that I will not get to share my life with him and discover what we could have been together. When I lost Tom, I lost everything. My whole life changed. I'm devastated right now, but I'm not lost like I was then."

"Well," said Jess. "I suppose that makes sense. You didn't know Krish as long as you knew Tom."

"It's more than that," said Kindra. "I actually feel bad for not feeling like my world just ended for the second time. I feel like I'm disrespecting Krish's memory."

"There is nothing wrong with the way you feel. No one can judge you for being sad or not being sad enough. You owe no one an explanation."

Alek felt like he was getting a first-hand lesson on love. The young elf had so little life experience with any relationship, let alone one of love. He understood Kindra had loved Krish, but also saw that her life was not dependent on his. Alek knew Tom was Kindra's first husband from the stories she had shared with him when she was Alek's prisoner. Kindra had described how they had built a life together when they were young. When Kindra lost Tom, she had never had a life without him. It hadn't only been Tom's love she had lost back then; it had been all they had created and experienced together.

Alek was also beginning to understand the love between Kindra and Jess. That love was more like the love between Kindra and Tom. The women's lives were woven together. If one were forced to continue on without the other, it would cause a terrible kind of heartache. Jess caught Alek watching her and Kindra. She offered him a smile.

"Why don't the two of you come over here? We're all sad, but we'll be alright if we share our pain together," said Jess.

Alek and Riva climbed off the bed and stood with Jess around Kindra. The three of them wrapped themselves around Kindra in a group hug. Daisy deigned to leave the comfort of the bed so she would not be left out. She wiggled her body into the center of the hug and put her front feet on Kindra's lap. Kindra found it impossible not to smile.

There was a knock at the door. The room's occupants looked up in concert and Jess called for the guest to enter. Syndral strode through the door and took in the scene. Jess was overwhelmed with guilt as she realized she and Kindra had shared the news about Krish with Riva without permission from Syndral. The correct action would have been to share the news with Syndral and then let Syndral handle it the way she desired. The guilt only became stronger as Jess realized that Syndral would not even be aware that Jess and Kindra had handled the situation inappropriately.

Jess tugged Kindra to her feet and gave her a little push toward the door. As Jess followed behind Kindra, she paused very close to Syndral. She confirmed Krish's death in a whisper to the warrior and suggested that Syndral talk about it with Riva. The young elf had not said a word during Kindra's emotional display, and Jess was concerned that the girl might need some guidance after what she had witnessed.

Jess followed Kindra through the doorway, and Alek watched Syndral approach the bed. Riva scooted to the side so her mother could sit down and pet Daisy. For a moment, all three of them stroked the dog's fur. Daisy, rolling over, enjoyed the pets now that she was once again in her prime location at the center of the bed. Syndral inhaled deeply and slowly released the air, as if she were preparing herself for battle.

"Ok, Alek," Syndral said. "I need to have a talk with Riva. Do you mind giving us a little time together?"

Jess, Kindra and Syndral were sitting at the large table in the kitchen several hours later. Einar had prepared Kindra's favorite, pheasant stew, as comfort food. Kindra was grateful for the stew and the support of Einar and the others, but she was confused. Kindra was waiting for grief to crash over her. When her first husband, Tom, had passed away, her world had fallen apart. The anguish had been something she could actually taste. The dull ache she felt now didn't feel like enough. *Maybe it is too soon for me to have internalized a love deep enough to cause that kind of angst over Krish's loss?*

Kindra and Tom were only married for eight months, but they had been together for several years before their wedding. Their lives were completely entwined and Tom's death had left Kindra feeling as if she did not know who she was without him. Kindra felt sad over Krish, but she didn't feel broken. *This must be shock. I'll feel lost soon enough.*

Joral and Gunnar came through the servants' door at the same time Mildred entered through the main doorway. Mildred carried a large wool blanket and wrapped it around Kindra's shoulders. Joral watched Mildred's gentle nicety and lowered his head.

"I guess you received the news," said Joral. "I'm so sorry, Kindra."

"I'm sorry too," Kindra replied. "You and Gunnar knew him longer than I have been alive. Mildred, Einar... I'm sorry for your loss, as well. He spent more time at Millspare than Gulentine Palace, and you basically raised Krish. Really, you all need to stop fussing over me. You have experienced a loss as great as, or greater than mine."

"It doesn't mean we can't be here for you," said Gunnar.

"Fine," said Kindra. "You are all here for me and I appreciate it. Unfortunately, some of that will need to wait. Imra is in the dungeon. She arrived, while you were searching for Tobias, to tell us Ulford is dead and some kind of fairy godmother guided her here to beg for our help in stopping Skilanis from destroying the realms."

Kindra was not sorry for the way she dropped the news on the princes. Allowing the words to spill from her had the effect of distracting everyone from treating her as though she were fragile, as well as giving her thoughts new direction. She would much rather be creating a plan of action than wallowing in the pity of others.

Joral schooled his expression. "I assume Leif went home to the human realm after... well... did Leif leave after telling you what happened?"

"He came to tell me Krish was dead and that he caused it. He admitted to taking Trego's drugs before it happened. As punishment, I sent Trego back to Gulentine and had Leif locked up in the cell next to Imra. I'm sure they are entertaining each other as we speak."

"Good, I think? Leif left before I shared what Tobias said as he died. Alek is in danger," said Joral.

"It looks like we all have a lot to share. Gunnar, I know you are new to this fatherhood thing, but you might want to sit this one out and go speak to your kid. Alek didn't know Krish well, but death can affect children in different ways. You need to be sure he gets any questions answered, and that he knows he can talk to you if he needs to speak about it," said Kindra.

"I trust your judgement as a psychologist, Kindra, but I have been a father for less than twenty-four hours. It might be better if

Syndral speaks to Alek at the same time she discusses death with Riva."

Syndral smirked. "Valiant effort, Gunnar. You won't be escaping your responsibilities that easily. I spoke to Riva earlier. You're on your own."

Gunnar sighed. "How did the talk with Riva go? Do you have any pointers?"

"It went," said Syndral. "It's not like I've been parenting much longer than you have. I hardly think I should give advice. Good luck."

CHAPTER 15

King Erik trembled as he kneeled before his own throne. He pressed his eyes closed against the nightmare surrounding him. Nothing had seemed amiss when Erik had entered Gulentine Palace from the garden. His escorts had taken leave of him once he was safely behind the palace walls. Two members of the Royal Guard had accompanied the King to his throne room to begin the monotony of the day. Before setting foot inside the great hall that housed the throne and served as an audience chamber, the heads of his two personal guards had rolled to the ground. Erik had reached for his sword, only to have his scabbard sliced from his belt by the guards' murderer. King Erik was shoved into the throne room.

The sight of the disemboweled people strewn throughout the large chamber burned in King Erik's mind. Though his eyes were shut tight, he still saw images of soldiers and citizens pinned to the ground with wolf-like creatures atop them. The beasts were feasting on the bodies of the dead.

"Open your eyes, your Highness," said the assailant. "Come on now. It seems rude for us to have a conversation without looking each other in the eye."

King Erik allowed his eyes to open, but he refused to look around the room. He stared straight back into the eyes of the man now sitting on the Throne of Lillerem.

"Sitting on that chair does not make you the king," Erik spat.

"No, unfortunately, it is not that easy, is it? Even if I kill you, I can't just sit here and decree that I am the new ruler of the Kingdom.

That would have been a page out of Ulford's playbook. I still argue that he was a king in name only. I'm not even sure the Kingdom of Dredfall was a real country. Everyone just seemed to accept it as one," said the male on the throne.

"If not the throne, what is it you want?" asked Erik.

"Oh, I never said I didn't want the throne, but let's not get ahead of ourselves. I am Skilanis. You might recognize my name and know me to be one of Ulford's assassins. I used to be a member of his Elite Guard."

"Used to be? I guess even Ulford didn't want you anymore?" asked the King.

"If Ulford were still alive, I can assure you he would want me on his side. Unfortunately, he and I had a difference of opinion on how to gain the most power."

"So you took Ulford's throne out from under him, and now you're coming for the throne of Lillerem. Very original. Ulford didn't succeed and neither will you," Erik said bravely.

Skilanis smiled. "That is where Ulford and I differ. He lost focus on his goal. His objective was petty and small-minded, anyway. I am highly focused. When I am through, there will be no Dredfall. There will be no Lillerem. Every kingdom will be erased from the realm and I will control everything that survives the chaos. It will all be mine."

"Even if Ulford's army has sworn allegiance to you, you still don't command enough troops and munitions to defeat one kingdom, let alone all of them. You are out of your mind!"

Skilanis renewed his smile. "Look around you, Highness. I am but a single soldier, and your palace is now populated by corpses. I command an army of decay. I have no need for traditional soldiers."

In one motion, Skilanis rose to his feet and drew his sword through the air. Erik's head hit the floor. The King's body hesitated for a moment, as though carrying out a last act of defiance. Then King Erik's body toppled and joined the rest of the corpses.

It took Gunnar some time to locate Alek. It had been more than a hundred years since Gunnar was Alek's age, and he had forgotten how difficult it was to stay cooped up indoors. Gunnar had been surprised to feel something akin to panic when he found Riva alone in her chambers with Daisy. The girl said something about not having GPS tracking for Alek, and she did not know where he was. The only useful information Gunnar had taken away from his conversation with Riva was that he was happy he did not have an adolescent daughter.

There was no way Gunnar was going to climb into a tree. Alek, staring down from the branches above, had invited him up to the 'fort' the boy had hastily constructed. Even if Gunnar could have reached the flimsy wooden structure, it was impossible for it to support the weight of a full grown warrior. Gunnar was not entirely sure the construction was capable of supporting Alek.

"Time for play has ended for now, young one. Return your feet to the ground. We must speak," Gunnar commanded.

Alek cocked his head for a moment. His impulse was to remain in the tree and taunt Gunnar for not being able to climb up. It wasn't that Alek wished to see Gunnar fall. He had a burning need to show his father what he had been doing all morning. Alek was proud of his tree house. After a minute, Alek decided the smarter move would be to climb down and keep from stoking Gunnar's anger.

"Walk with me," Gunnar said as soon as Alek reached the forest floor.

Gunnar started off on the trail, winding back toward Millspare, leaving Alek to catch up. The pair walked in silence for a moment, taking in the sounds of nature as Gunnar gathered his thoughts, trying to decide how to approach the subject of death.

"Did you drag me down here to talk about Krish?" Alek asked.

Surprised, Gunnar asked, "What made you think that?"

"Syndral made me leave her and Riva alone this morning. When I went in for a snack later, I saw Riva and she told me her mother made her have a serious conversation about how people die and everything is better in the afterlife."

"She told you that, did she?" Gunnar asked.

"Yeah. Syndral told Riva that when a good person dies, they get to live forever in a place where nothing bad ever happens," said Alek.

"And? How do you feel about that?" Gunnar asked.

"It sounds good to me, but I'm not so sure it's true. I mean, who gets to decide if someone is good or not? Krish seemed really nice, but I don't think the mothers of all the soldiers he has killed would agree," Alek shared. "What do you think happens when we die?"

Gunnar grunted. "I think… it's complicated."

Alek felt the emotional turmoil hidden behind Gunnar's resigned exterior. Alek quickly realized he had been foolish with his words. Gunnar had killed a lot of people as well and he was not known as a jovial or kind person, even among those he was close with. Moreover, Gunnar's brother, Leif, was one of the least kind elves Alek had met, yet he had a good heart. The truth of his father's words sat heavily with Alek. It *was* complicated. Alek reached out to Gunnar as they walked. Wrapping his fingers around the middle three fingers of Gunnar's enormous hand, Alek squeezed. Gunnar moved his hand to take Alek's hand within his own.

"I was told to provide comfort for you in the face of Krish's death, but somehow, I feel it is you doing the comforting. Is there anything I can do for you?" asked Gunnar.

"Yes," said Alek. "I was mad at her when we were at Smalgroth, but now I feel bad about it. Do you think we can go talk to my mother?"

"Of course, that is the one thing you desire," Gunnar sighed. "You shall have it."

Imra had been foolish to think her sister would welcome her here with open arms and kisses. Even when she and Syndral were fighting on the same side, they had not always been civil to each other. When Imra had become the focus of Ulford's attention, Syndral had only been a foot soldier. Syndral's jealousy had quickly worn away any sisterly feelings she and Imra might have shared as children. Imra had not minded. Her time was consumed by leading Ulford on his quest to seize more power and rid the realms of anyone who might challenge him. In exchange, Imra had the coveted position beside the most callous and evil male in Alfheim. No one would challenge her authority, and Imra was taken care of and free to do as she pleased.

That had been her life until recently, anyway. Skilanis had proved to be a more evil and power-hungry male than Ulford ever was.

Ulford was content to rule over Dredfall and eventually neighboring kingdoms traditionally, if not kindly. Skilanis's plan to control Alfheim meant obliterating all current political systems. More specifically, Skilanis's methods for taking power over the realm required him to destroy Alfheim and then rebuild it as he desired. Imra wondered if Skilanis was planning for the possibility that there might not be any people left after the destruction of the realm. Was he unable to see the chance that might become reality, or did he not care? Was Skilanis so sure of himself and his plan that the risk of complete destruction of anything worth ruling over was not even a consideration?

Imra's attention was drawn to the cell next to her own. Prince Leif was waking from his nap. It was a bit of a comfort to Imra to know she was not the only sibling being held in the dungeon below Millspare. The elf groaned and stretched. He looked around his cell and sighed when his eyes landed on Imra. Imra raised her hand and gave Leif a tiny wave.

"Welcome to my humble abode," Imra said.

"You might think about dismissing your decorator. I'm fairly certain shades of gray went out of fashion several years ago. This place needs a splash of color," said Leif.

"I admit the cells lack the latest comforts, but I think you'll find meals are provided regularly and your basic needs will be met," said Imra.

"At least in the human realm you get to call a lawyer to post bail for you," Leif said.

"Call a what? Is 'post bail' a new term for murdering your captors?" asked Imra.

Leif chuckled. "You've actually never left this realm, have you?"

"No. Well, not for any length of time. I was perfectly happy where I was until recently," said Imra.

"Don't lie to him, Imra. Happy is not the word you should be using for how you felt about your life. Content maybe?" asked a voice Imra was beginning to know well.

Tomia stood outside of Imra's cell. The old female placed her hand on the lock of Imra's cage. There was a faint pulse of light and then a click. Imra's cell door swung open.

Leif cleared his throat. "Ahem. Do you think you can handle doing that one more time, love?"

"You can see her?" Imra asked in surprise.

"Of course he can see me," said Tomia. "If I were a figment of your imagination, I wouldn't be able to manipulate solid objects, would I?"

"I don't know," Imra answered. "I've never had a fairy godmother before."

"You still don't," snapped Tomia. "I do not belong to you, elf. I already told you I am doing what is needed to save the nine realms. You are only a puzzle piece."

Leif narrowed his eyes at Tomia as she moved to place her hand on the lock of his cell. The flash of light came again, and the door to Leif's cell clicked open. Leif analyzed the old female and slowly moved his gaze from her bare feet, up her burlap dress, and to her face. He let his eyes rest on Tomia's scarred cheek and empty eye socket.

Tomia starred back. "I see you have an interest in where Nidhogg took my eye. I put him in his place, and he was content with my roots from then on."

"I knew it," said Leif.

"Knew what?" asked Imra. "You two have met before?"

Tomia answered. "We've all been acquainted since you came to be. I am the source of life for all creatures and beings within the realms."

"You're a god?" Imra asked.

Tomia laughed. "Hardly. Even they would not exist without the life I breathe into them. Come now."

Tomia walked back down the dank hall toward the stone stairwell that led up to the main levels of Millspare. Imra was ready to follow when the elder elf dissipated into mist and was gone from sight.

"Tomia has been following me since I left Fallholm," Imra explained to Leif. "She helped me the night I fled Bindrell. She gave me food, cleaned me up and gave me clothes. Then, she let me rest in her shack. I saw her again when I made it through the Dredskog. I was dehydrated, and she brought me water. She has been protecting me throughout my entire journey."

"I doubt she did any of that as a favor to you," Leif replied.

"Who is she? I can tell you know her. If she wasn't helping me, then why did she do all those things for me?"

"You didn't read much as a child, did you?" asked Leif.

"No. Not really."

"I don't think Tomia is a who. I am almost positive she is a what," said Leif. "As she said, it's not you she is here to help. It is her job to protect all the realms, not just Alfheim. Whatever is going on is much bigger than any of us know. I find it hard to believe she expects us to be much help if she is mounting a defense against a threat so large."

"It's starting to sound like those drugs you took haven't had a chance to wear off," said Imra. "Just tell me what's going on. You can leave out the mysticism and fairy tales, please."

"Fairy tales?" asked Leif. "You're the one who thought she was your fairy godmother! I have my suspicions, but I honestly have no idea what's happening. She's going to gather the others, though. Let's get upstairs so we don't miss the part where she explains herself… if she explains herself."

CHAPTER 16

Gunnar had to admit he felt happy. He was riding through the Lillerem countryside with his son. This was something he had never expected to experience. Gunnar kept glancing at the boy on the horse beside him. Alek's golden eyes were identical to Gunnar's. It was like looking at his own younger self. The freckles running across the bridge of the boy's nose were Frida's, though. Gunnar remembered warm evenings in the fields and frosty nights by the fire where he stared at Frida, memorizing her features and trying to count her freckles.

Gunnar sighed. He had failed Frida when it had mattered most. She had needed his support, and he had not been there. Anger started to overshadow the guilt within Gunnar. Frida had kept her pregnancy from Gunnar. If she had told him, he never would have left her to struggle on her own. Gunnar took a deep breath to help get his emotions under control. Alek might be ready to see his mother, but Gunnar was still struggling.

Alek's horse was keeping up well with Gunnar's stallion. Her name was Marbles, and Alek already loved her. Alek loved the way the wind pinned back his hair and his eyes teared a little from the same. Marble's motion felt effortless, and Alek trusted her to carry him safely and swiftly. Not for the first time, Alek wondered if he would ever trust a person in the same way he implicitly trusted animals. This made Alek even more thankful for his new gift. Alek had always taken what people said to him at face value. Many times, this had left him disappointed, or even in danger, due to people lying or deceiving him. Alek's gift could save him from that now, even if it was shocking how often a person's words did not match the person's emotions or intent.

Alek no longer needed to try to extend his magic to read someone's feelings. He felt it in the same way he used his sense of smell. It was always there, but his brain only registered changes or warnings when things weren't as they should be. In the same way Alek would sense the smell of smoke, he felt Gunnar's feelings roiling beside him. His father was fighting an internal battle between sorrow and rage. His emotions were sliding between the two in a perpetually changing combination of both feelings.

"How do you feel about seeing my mother?" Alek asked to test the waters.

"Fine. I'm glad you will be able to speak to her," Gunnar answered.

Gunnar's expression had not changed an iota, but his inner torment washed over Alek. It was Alek's turn to fight a battle of emotions. He really wanted to see Frida and have the chance to speak to her calmly. Alek wanted to understand her feelings and her reasons for choosing not to raise him. Fulfilling this desire meant that he was causing his father pain. Gunnar was not ready to talk to Frida. The show Gunnar was putting on for Alek made the boy smile. His father wanted him to be happy and was willing to experience his own pain to make that happen.

The pair rode into Smalgroth ten minutes later. They hadn't spoken once Alek had realized Gunnar was not excited about the journey. Alek reminded himself there had been fleeting feelings of contentment from Gunnar as well. Something about this trip was causing Gunnar a taste of happiness, at least. Gunnar settled both horses in at the stable and he and Alek walked back out onto the road. Frida ran down the steps of Kanin's house and greeted Gunnar and Alek, breathlessly.

"You need to come inside," Frida said. "Bane is here. You need to hear what he saw at Gulentine when he took Krish's body to…"

Frida let her sentence trail off, deciding action would be faster than words. Frida turned and jogged back to the house, skipping the three steps and jumping directly to the wooden porch. Gunnar and Alek, spurred by Frida's urgency, followed close behind her.

Bane and Kanin were at Kanin's large table. They looked up when Frida led Gunnar and Alek into the room. Alek felt fear from Gunnar. Gunnar was looking at Bane and all the color was leached from Bane's face. Of all the warriors Alek had met, Bane was the only one who displayed less emotion than Gunnar, and Bane's pale visage showed defeat.

"What the hell happened?" Gunnar asked.

To Alek, Gunnar didn't sound like he really wanted an answer. Potent emotions pushed at Alek from Bane. Bane was terrified.

"Death is coming. The king is dead. There is nothing left of Lillerem City. There is nothing to be done. Skilanis is too powerful."

"This is everyone," said Kindra. "Bane is in Gulentine and Gunnar is off gallivanting with his new son. I don't know where they are, so just start talking."

Tomia looked down her nose at Kindra from where she stood at the head of the table. Kindra sat in the seat to Tomia's left, trying to remain in control of the meeting but slowly accepting that the show belonged to the older female. Jess, Leif, Mildred, and Joral sat waiting for the promised announcement. Syndral and Imra stared at each other across the table, seething. Butch and Cassidy sat on either side of Einar, who was quickly preparing snacks on the other side of the kitchen. Viktor and Ruth sat reluctantly at the foot of the table, wearing identical looks of impassivity. Ruth adjusted a panel of her flowing gown where it pooled around her toes. It was the only sign that she was even remotely uncomfortable being summoned to her kitchen by a stranger.

"Bane is no longer in Gulentine. He has joined Gunnar and the boy in Smalgroth. They will not make it back here in time. We shall begin once our last guest arrives," Tomia announced.

Before anyone at the table gathered the nerve to ask who the missing member of the party could be, Tomia cocked her head. Everyone waited with anticipation for someone to come through the door. Tomia smiled and her gaze landed on the middle of the wall, to the left of the table.

"There is no need to spy, young one. Come join us."

Kindra concluded the elderly female was speaking to ghosts. There was no one standing next to the table. It looked as if Tomia had been talking directly to the stone wall. Whatever information was about to be shared in this room was going to be far from trustworthy. Kindra was about to stand from the table and refuse to take part in the discussion when Riva came through the main doorway.

"It didn't take long for her to find the listening passages," Mildred said under her breath.

Lowering her voice hadn't helped in the silence of the room. Everyone at the table had heard Mildred. Einar did not try to hide the smile on his face when he saw the look of astonishment on Viktor's face.

"Listening passages?" Ruth prompted.

Mildred smiled. "If you were less of a proper young lady, it is likely you would have discovered them for yourself when you were younger. It seems our little Riva has a lot to learn about propriety and manners, though."

Riva took the seat next to her mother. Cassidy immediately abandoned his task of patrolling the floor for any scraps dropped by Einar and took a position lying across Riva's feet under the table.

"Before you start…" Leif had been staring at Tomia the whole time she was in the room. "Are you Yggdrasil?"

Joral laughed loudly. "The ash tree from the fairy tales? You must have a stash of Trego's tincture. That's ridiculous."

Tomia directed a soft smile to Leif. Her eyes were kind. The look was similar to that of a mother looking down at her newborn. A moment later, her expression hardened, and she turned her attention back to everyone in the room.

"Welcome. You are the last line of defense for Alfheim. The fate of all nine realms rests on your ability to defend it. If you fail, life everywhere will cease to exist."

"No pressure," Leif said under his breath.

Tomia continued as if she hadn't heard. "Skilanis intends to seize control of more than Lillerem. He desires all of Alfheim for his own. Riva is the key to his entire plan."

"She's what?" Syndral shouted. "She's a child. How can she be part of the destruction of an entire realm?"

"You mistake my words," said Tomia. "She will not be responsible for the destruction of Alfheim. If Skilanis uses her as he desires, Riva will be responsible for the destruction of all nine realms."

"This is ridiculous!" Syndral said.

Standing from her seat, Syndral started to pull Riva from hers. "There is no way I'm going to let my daughter sit here and listen to some crazy old elf tell her she will bring the destruction of the nine realms."

Riva grasped the edge of the table. The room, previously close to stifling from the burning fire, went cold. Frost formed on the floor at Syndral's feet. Cassidy backed away from the area, but didn't bother to get up and run.

"I'm not a child, mother," Riva said calmly. "Technically, I am older than Jess and Kindra. I'm tired of people sheltering me as if I were a human infant. I'll stay and listen to what Tomia has to tell us."

Syndral, with no power to rebuff her daughter's magic, released Riva. For once, Imra was not glaring at her sister. There was pity in Imra's eyes as Syndral returned to her seat. Teenage elves were notoriously difficult to control, but one as powerful as Riva was likely to kill someone during a tantrum, even if it was her own mother.

"Please, continue telling us how poor, innocent Riva could possibly be the cause of the destruction of the realms," said Leif.

"As you know," Tomia said, "Skilanis has collected his pets by pulling creatures from the realm of Niflheim. The creatures there are pulled to our realm easily with the right mixture of bones from a certain combination of realms. Skilanis found he could satisfy the requirements of the magic if the bones came from beings born of both human and Elven ancestry. Individual bones harvested from humans with Elven blood made it possible for Skilanis to draw creatures from Niflheim at an unfathomable rate. He currently has an entire army of the dead."

"How do you propose we stop this army?" Jess asked.

"You don't," Tomia answered. "There is no way to stop an army of the dead that has already reached this size."

"So why are we even here?" asked Syndral. "If all is lost, what are we supposed to do?"

"You all have a role to play. The goal is to prevent Skilanis from getting the last thing he needs in order to pull a World Destroyer from the realm of fire. He is missing the final ingredient for his bone mixture. We will use the precise item he desires to lure him in. Once he is there, your combined abilities will hold back his army of the dead while we wait for the arrival of the Vanir God who will put an end to Skilanis's march of destruction."

"What makes you so sure he will fall for our trap?" asked Joral. "If we can't stop his army, he could just parade across Lillerem until he has destroyed every square inch of it."

"Skilanis has already started his march. The destruction of Lillerem City has come to pass. It took several hours. Skilanis does not have the patience to repeat the process throughout the kingdom, let alone throughout the realm. With the acquisition of the final prerequisite, Skilanis will pull the World Destroyer from Muspelheim and he will have control of Alfheim in minutes. What he fails to understand, is that his actions will disrupt the balance between the nine realms. With this realm destroyed, the other realms will cease to exist as well," explained Tomia.

"You said we needed a Vanir God to stop Skilanis and his army?" asked Kindra. "If you hold the realms together and supply life within them or whatever, why didn't you just go to them and ask the Gods to stop Skilanis?"

"It's not that simple," said Tomia. "Since the cease-fire between realms was put in place, the Gods of both Asgard and Vanaheim refuse to take part in the governance of other realms. I spoke with leaders among the giants and trolls of Jötunheim, as well as dwarves from Nidavellir. All thanked me for the warning, but felt they were better off using their forces to defend their own realm than sending armies to fight in Alfheim. I did not bother with a trip to Svartalfheim. If the dwarves and giants would not come to your aid, then the dark elves surely won't. They are the least compassionate, sentient beings in the realms. Representatives of the only two realms with beings empathetic enough to care for the fate of all nine realms are in this room. As I said, you are the last hope for Alfheim."

"You just said the Vanir Gods refuse to interfere in the governance of other realms. Why would they change their minds and join us to complete your plan?" Joral challenged.

"We only need one," answered Tomia. "He'll come to protect his daughter."

Tomia leveled her gaze at Riva. The girl's eyes grew to the size of saucers while Syndral's eyes turned to fire.

"That was not information for you to share!" Syndral spat.

"I didn't say a word," replied Tomia calmly. "Besides, I said Riva was the key to this entire operation. She's not just the reason we'll have our Vanir God. She's also the reason we'll be able to lure Skilanis."

"What is the final thing Skilanis needs to summon his world-ending being from the realm of fire?" Syndral said through clenched teeth.

"Skilanis is hunting for the unfused bones of the skull of an Elven child. That child needs to be exceptionally powerful. I thought we had suspended the inevitable when Riva was hidden here at Millspare, but Skilanis is unknowingly going to find her, anyway. It will be a mistake, of sorts, as he pursues a different child," Tomia admitted.

"Forgive me, Tomia," interrupted Jess. "I mean no disrespect, but how are you sure that the pursuit of some other kid is going to lead Skilanis to Riva?"

"While in Dredfall, Skilanis heard of a child who was able to move objects with his mind. Children with powers are rare in Alfheim. Only powerful children manifest magic like that before they come of age. Skilanis tracked the young elf into the Dredskog when he ran away."

Kindra stopped Tomia by holding up her hand. "You're telling us Skilanis is currently chasing after Alek? Alek, who is presently half-way to Gulentine with Gunnar, in Smalgroth?"

"Unfortunately, yes," answered Tomia. "You will need to leave as soon as possible."

"I think you really should have led with that part of your announcement," said Jess.

"If I had done that, you never would have stayed to hear the information that explained what you are up against," replied Tomia.

"Not knowing what we are up against has never stopped us before. We need to ride for Smalgroth," Kindra said.

Everyone stood from the table to begin hurriedly packing gear and readying horses; everyone except Syndral. Jess paused as she approached Syndral on her way out of the kitchen.

"I noticed you haven't moved," Jess said.

"Riva and I will be staying behind."

"Have you discussed that with Riva?" Jess asked.

"There is no need for a discussion," Syndral answered. "She is a child. She may have been alive as long as you have, but that is a fraction of an elven life. I will not allow her to be put in danger. We can do this another way."

"What do you propose? Are you planning to pick up the phone and call your ex? It seems like drawing whoever he is to the location of the battle is a big part of making this plan work," taunted Jess.

"I suppose this is the part where I'm supposed to tell you how Riva ended up with a God for a father?"

"I am dying to know the answer to that mystery, and I suspect your daughter is curious as well. It might be a good story for the ride to Smalgroth. I know you think you're staying, but Riva is a teenage elf. It would not surprise me if she already had a horse saddled and ready. Instead of putting your foot down, you might consider getting both of your feet moving, if you intend to be with her when she needs your help," said Jess.

CHAPTER 17

It hadn't taken Bane long to share his news with Gunnar and Alek. Not one to use more words than necessary, Bane had Gunnar up-to-date in less than five minutes, once they had all been seated at Kanin's table. Bane had met Trego on the way to the palace, and the two had accompanied Krish's body to Gulentine together. Upon arrival, they had seen the utter destruction left in the wake of Skilanis's incursion. Trego remained behind to oversee the burial of the King and the Crown Prince, as well as to help tend to the healing of any survivors. It had been chance that Gunnar and Alek arrived at Smalgroth around the same time as Bane. Bane was headed to Millspare to raise the alarm.

Kanin had been a runner for the Lillerem army when he was a younger elf. He could still outpace any horse with the use of his magic. He had run for the first neighboring village as soon as Bane had finished his story. It would be Kanin's job to send as many civilians south, out of Skilanis's current path of devastation, as possible. Gunnar, Bane, Alek and Frida were riding for Millspare.

Unlike Kanin, who was looking to provide as early a warning as possible, the group was not rushed. While in Lillerem City, Bane had heard that Skilanis's army of the dead took time to move. Though the hundespor could cover ground quickly, the army could only move as one if it maintained the pace of its slowest creatures. The merknifol preferred to travel in darkness, and the frost giants were slowed by the heat of the sun.

Bane rode point, followed by Gunnar. This allowed Alek and Frida some semblance of privacy.

"I'm sorry I ran out of your kitchen," said Alek. "I was just upset. I didn't realize we'd leave Smalgroth and I wouldn't see you later."

"I don't think it is you who should be offering up apologies," said Frida. "I put my own needs and the needs of your grandmother ahead of yours. It was a decision that cost you your childhood."

"I still got a childhood," Alek laughed. "Not having parents doesn't keep you from getting to be a kid."

"That's not exactly what I meant," replied Frida. "I know you don't know any other way, but I know you would have had a more enjoyable life if you had not been raised as a slave."

"You don't need to worry. I had an enjoyable childhood. I got to play football and other games with lots of other kids. It wasn't anything like what they did to the adults," Alek argued.

Frida smiled sadly. "I'm really not sure if you just don't know any better, or you're trying to make me feel less guilty. Either way, you need to stop defending slavery. Whether they allowed you to play with the other children or not, life as a slave is not a life. You were owned as property, and that is unacceptable."

"It's not like it was you who treated me that way. You don't need to be so sad about it," said Alek.

"I think I do," replied Frida. "I was so set on the idea that life with me would not be a good life that I failed to think about how much worse it could be. When my neighbor told me he knew someone who wanted a child, I didn't even ask questions. I should have at least met the people who claimed to want you. I don't even know if it was the neighbor who sold you to Ulford or if he was simply unaware that you would be sold by people he trusted."

"See, you just said you didn't know," said Alek. "It's not your fault."

"I didn't know then, but once I got my life back together, I never tried to find you."

"You wouldn't have been able to find me," Alek said.

"But I didn't even try," replied Frida.

"I know I'm not as old as you are, but I think you've got things all mixed up. At first I was mad you didn't want me, but once you gave me up, there was nothing you could do. The person you could have told, and should be talking with, is riding up there."

Frida's eyes shifted to Gunnar's back. Alek could feel her emotions jumping from within her. She was terrified, but there was love in there too. Alek cocked his head in Gunnar's direction to urge Frida on. She continued to ride beside Alek. Changing tactics, Alek rode up beside Gunnar and told him Frida wanted to speak with him. Frida's eyes went wide as she realized what her sneaking offspring had done. Alek turned his head to the front as he rode beside Bane.

"Does Frida have magic?" Alek asked.

Bane sighed, as if speaking was a nuisance. "Yes."

"What can she do?" Alek asked.

"She can hold things in place."

Alek tried to listen in on the conversation behind him, but Gunnar and Frida were speaking in whispers. They were quite a bit farther back than Alek and Frida had been riding when Gunnar was up front with Bane. Alek imagined his mother's power would be very useful for leather crafts. Being able to hold things in place would be equivalent to having an extra pair of hands while she worked.

"Do you have magic?" Alek asked.

"No," Bane replied. "My mother was a troll. Her blood suppressed any magic I might have manifested."

"I guess you don't really need magic," Alek said. "I don't think I've ever met anyone as strong as you are."

"You should have met my mother," Bane replied.

"No thank you," said Alek. "From what I've heard, trolls sometimes kill people by accident because they are so strong. I've even heard they sometimes kill their own—"

Alek stopped speaking mid-sentence. The clouds off in the distance on his right had caught his attention. When Alek pulled on his horse's reins, Marbles slowed to a stop. Bane followed Alek's gaze toward the horizon and turned his horse to face the strange sight. There was an angry storm in the distance. Gunnar and Frida caught up to Alek and Bane as the first two riders continued to watch the storm clouds closing the distance across the plain.

"I've never seen anything like that before," said Frida. "What kind of storm makes clouds like that?"

Gunnar, the only one in the group who had ever traveled to the human realm, felt his heart rate pick up. Though he had never experienced clouds that looked like those quickly approaching, he had watched weather shows on Leif's television. The dark clouds appeared to touch the ground. They were like bricks in a large, dark gray wall. Gunnar looked closer as he tried to determine if the wall looked like it was rotating.

"It reminds me of videos I've seen of tornadoes," Gunnar said. "I don't think it's a tornado, though. It is far too wide, and the debris would be rotating very quickly. This looks more like a wall of black dust that is rolling toward us."

"Not dust," said Bane. "It's mist."

Once Gunnar said the word, Alek could see that the gray wall was, indeed, a dense mist. It was more like a single giant cloud and it appeared to be covering ground at an alarming rate. Without a word, Bane kicked his horse into a gallop and headed for the tree-line at the top of the hill before them. Gunnar, Frida, and Alek did the same. The horses struggled to gain ground as the group took the incline head-on.

As if the mist knew where it wanted to go, the entire dark cloud changed direction. The darkness was no longer rolling across the plain and farmland. It was pushing straight toward the group of four riders as they struggled to climb the steep rise. Bane, the heaviest of them by at least a hundred pounds, started to fall behind. Between Bane's weight on her back and the arduous climb, his mare was quickly slowing. Alek watched over his shoulder as Bane jumped from his horse and turned to face the oncoming mist. Bane's horse, hundreds of pounds lighter, shot up the hill, now able to escape the wall of darkness.

Gunnar was the next to dismount. To say Alek was confused would be an understatement. There was no way either warrior would be able to fight the darkness. Mist could not be killed with a sword or dagger. Alek felt sick as he realized what Bane, and then his father, had done. They were sacrificing themselves to whatever evil was driving the dark cloud up the hill. Gunnar's last words before he was swallowed by the cloud confirmed Alek's fears.

"Go, Alek! As fast as you can! Get to the top!"

Alek and Frida were much lighter than either warrior, but a quick look behind Alek told him they would be cutting it close. They might actually reach the top before they were swallowed by the mist, but then what? If this hill didn't stop the rolling cloud, then the trees at the top wouldn't either. If anything, the trees would limit Alek and Frida's speed, but allow the mist to continue unimpeded.

A beam of light shot over Alek's head from the top of the hill. Startled, Marbles reared and threw Alek to the ground. He rolled down the hill a few feet before he felt himself stick to the ground. Frida was at his side in seconds. She grabbed his hands and yanked him to his feet. The two of them started running up the hill until they reached the outstretched arms of...

"Joral? What are you doing here?" Alek asked.

"We're all here," Joral replied.

He turned to run the rest of the way up the hill, but Alek's left foot was glued to the ground again. Alek looked toward Frida, who had remounted her horse and continued up the hill. She was not holding him in place. Alek felt a tug, and his hand slipped from Joral's. Alek turned to look behind him as he started to slide backward down the hill. A tendril of mist, wrapped around his foot, was making its way up his leg. No, that was not mist. Another dark, snake-like creature grabbed Alek's other ankle. Langen were pulling him into the dark cloud.

Darkness engulfed Alek. He knew Joral was only feet away, but Alek could no longer see him. The langen dragged him deeper into the mist. Alek felt forms pushing on him from all sides. He was not being dragged straight along the ground. He felt his body moving up and down over solid objects, then falling slightly through cool air, only to bump against another obstacle. The journey was nauseating.

<hr>

Riva watched Alek slide down the hill, langen twisting up his legs. The horse Alek had been riding left him behind and ran for the hilltop. Riva had a view of the entire valley from her perch, high in a tree, set back several hundred feet from where the edge of the forest met the steep grassy area that led to the valley below. She closed her eyes and let her magic flow from deep within her. Riva took care to pin herself close to the trunk of her tree as she conjured wind, but no storm.

At the base of the tree, feet firmly planted on the ground, Imra moved behind the massive trunk and took hold as she felt Riva's magic begin to whip around her. Imra had been able to use her magic to bring the group to the exact location they would need to be if they had any chance of surviving the conflict that was now beginning. The only thing she could do now was stay alive.

Syndral stood next to Joral. They both held their swords in front of them, but neither of them had advanced when Alek was pulled into the mist. The mist had halted just before reaching Joral. Syndral had poked it with the tip of her sword and it had only swirled in the air. Neither of them had any idea how to attack a cloud. Syndral felt a breeze lift her hair from the back of her neck. Looking over her shoulder, the tug in her heart drew her eyes up to where her daughter sat watching from the branches of a tall tree. The breeze picked up and became wind.

Syndral tied her hair out of her face with a strip of leather and turned to face forward where the mist was being pushed back down the hill. Immediately, Syndral wished the mist had remained in place.

The army of the dead stood revealed. A frost giant swung its fist at Syndral and she swung her sword to remove its arm. Spinning, she continued the arc of the sword to bring the blade back through the creature's neck. Cold blood sprayed and the creature's head fell to the ground. Horrifying though the sight was, at least now they could see the enemy, including the merknifol retreating with the mist to avoid the sunlight.

From the top of the hill, bursts of light began flying from Leif's hands. The beams of light sent into the hoard barreled through several enemies before dissipating. Each thrust of Leif's hands took down three or four soldiers from the army of the dead. Frida saw the opportunity this presented. The next time Leif fired his light into the army of the dead, the beam killed five soldiers that had been glued into the light's path. Leif, having felt the pulse of power from his left and seen the soldiers fail to move out of his light's path, nodded at Frida in appreciation. She moved closer to Leif so they could combine their power in more coordinated attacks.

Kindra's eyes roamed the field of battle and met disappointment, again. She kept searching for Krish to see if he needed help, and then had to remind herself he wouldn't be there. She spotted Bane and Gunnar, several yards deep into the fray, standing back to back as they took down frost giants and sliced through langen.

Kindra closed her eyes and envisioned stasis around the two males. When Kindra opened her eyes, the evil soldiers within a ten-foot radius of Gunnar and Bane stood still. Gunnar paused a moment as he processed the event, but Bane did not miss a beat. He went from hacking down attacking beasts to hacking down statues as if he had expected them to freeze in place all along.

Langen were the first to attempt crossing into the circle of unmoving foes. They moved freely through the legs of their frozen counterparts. Seeing the fur covered serpents remain mobile through the circle of stillness, frost giants started to advance once again. Merknifol started to emerge from the mist, braving the sunlight after they overcame their initial hesitation. Kindra closed her eyes again. This time, she pictured the entire army of the dead freezing in place. She opened her eyes, expecting to see she had essentially frozen time, similar to the effect of freezing the soldiers when Millspare had been attacked several months ago.

Kindra was frustrated to find she did not have the ability to pull off such a feat. Stopping these other-worldly creatures in their tracks required more strength. Kindra would need to settle for precise strikes in the vicinity of Gunnar and Bane to help them work their way through the crush of the dead.

Jess stood at the top of the hill, a little to the right and just behind Leif and Frida, as they coordinated their assault. Jess felt helpless. She had tried to enter the minds of the creatures that made up the dead army in front of her, but these creatures did not belong to her power. Butch sat to Jess's left, and Cassidy to her right. The dogs were filled with the same nervous anticipation as Jess while they waited for direction from her. Jess was not about to send her dogs into the fight, knowing they would be overrun almost immediately.

Jess closed her eyes and reached her mind out to the forested area behind her. She moved telepathically through every animal she encountered. *Rabbits, deer, birds... birds!* At least now she had an idea. The sounds of squawking and beating wings grew louder as Jess's flock grew in size and approached the hilltop from the trees. The sun was blocked from the land for a moment as thousands of birds emerged from the trees and set their sights on the enemy spread across the hillside and part of the valley below. Crows, hawks, ravens, and many species Jess did not have names for dove at the soldiers, driving their beaks into the softest tissue. Eyes were plucked from giants, and langen were pulled from the fight and carried off into the sky.

Had this been an army of the living, the birds would have been an overwhelming distraction. The frost giants did not need their eyes, and the number of langen the birds carried off barely reduced the size of the cohort. Jess called off the birds as soon as she saw they were having little effect. She did not want innocent animals to die because of her. What she really needed were some bears or something big like that, but they were solitary creatures, for the most part. A herd of buffalo might trample the creatures below her, but it didn't seem like there were any in Alfheim. Jess took a deep breath and reached out into the world around her once again.

She felt something big and followed the mental thread. Whatever it was, there were more than one of them and they were flying in this direction. The strength of the creatures had to be colossal because they were still miles away, but Jess could feel them. She couldn't communicate with them at this distance, but they were growing closer. They were not part of the army of the dead, but Jess wasn't sure if the creatures were friend or foe. She continued to try to call to them through her mental bond.

Riva had the best vantage point to see the moment when the direction of the battle started to turn. The number of evil creatures was lessening. It no longer looked like a dark horde on the hill below. Instead, Riva could see the individual combats as they unfolded. Gunnar and Bane were farthest from her position. They had fought their way out of the thick of battle to the perimeter all the way to the right. Jess stood above them on the hill. Frida and Leif were working together to hold back the dead army, so that Syndral and Joral would not be overrun as they felled attackers before them. Syndral held her hand against her side and looked to be having trouble keeping her feet beneath her body. They were making progress, but it was obvious they were tiring.

Riva allowed herself to look out deeper into the army of the dead and down to the soldiers still in the valley below. She felt her heart plummet when she finally laid eyes on Alek. From her position at the top of the hill, Jess must have seen the boy just before Riva did. Butch and Cassidy took off down the hill.

The German Shepherd dogs dodged a few remaining frost giants and leaped over squirming langen. Thankfully, there no longer seemed to be merknifol among the members of the dead army. The creatures had been easy targets as the mist receded. The dogs were definitely on course to where the creepiest-looking elf Riva had ever seen held Alek in the air by an ankle. Alek swung his fists and squirmed to get free, but the forbidding elf only laughed. Alek was no threat to him.

Riva decided she would probably be laughing as well if she had a pack of hundespor sitting at her side, waiting for a command to attack. The wolf-like creatures looked bored. They had not even entered the fight.

Jess was on the move. She had her sword drawn and was cutting her way toward Alek. Her progress was slower than Butch and Cassidy's, but she was on her way.

Riva began to descend from the safety of her tree. Imra was hit with a small piece of bark kicked loose by Riva's boot.

"Don't you dare!" Imra screamed up at Riva. "You need to stay put!"

Riva reached the ground. She gave Imra a lopsided smile and waited for Imra to realize there was not a thing the older elf could do to stop Riva from entering the fight.

⁕⁕⁕

Alek took another swing at Skilanis. Using his magic, he picked up a small rock and sent it in the direction of Skilanis's head. It missed. Alek hurled another rock, and Skilanis used Alek's body to block the stone.

"Is this all you've got?" Skilanis snarled. "I should feel the power flowing from within you. Defend your life, boy!"

Alek continued to kick out with the leg Skilanis was not grasping. The blood had rushed to his head some time ago, and it throbbed now. *What is this vile elf waiting for?*

"I don't know who you think I am, but this has gone far enough. Put me down, or kill me already!" Alek yelled up at the Slave Master.

"You are the orphan child of a powerful being. I can't believe it escaped my notice when I had you working at the kennels. Your father, like my pets, is from another realm. The power he gifted to you will bring forth my World Destroyer."

Alek stopped squirming. Skilanis truly did not know who Alek was. The Slave Master had him confused with some other young elf. If this moment had occurred weeks, or even days ago, Alek would have been worried, but now the majority of his fear dissipated.

"Why didn't you just say so?" Alek asked incredulously. "You have the wrong kid. I know who my father is. He isn't from another realm. He lived in the human realm for a while, but he was born here. My father is strong and a powerful warrior, but he has no special magic."

Skilanis dropped Alek. Thankfully, Alek was able to get his hands under his head before the impact. It wasn't until Skilanis pulled the sword from his scabbard that Alek realized his impulsivity had put him in more danger. Skilanis no longer had need of Alek. This was exactly the point the young elf had been trying to prove, but doing so had just made Alek expendable.

A hundespor was launched from its feet by something crashing into its flank. The wolf-like beast came to rest inches from Alek. The German Shepherd dog atop it tore out the beast's throat. Skilanis whirled to his right where another dog had taken down a second hundespor. The Slave Master roared in pain as the first dog leaped from a downed hundespor and attacked Skilanis, going for his face. The other dog latched on to Skilanis's legs. Alek still could not tell the dogs apart on sight, but he was aware Butch and Cassidy had come to his rescue. The hundespor defended their master, and it did not take long before both German Shepherd dogs were ripped from Skilanis's form. Butch and Cassidy were outnumbered and outsized, but they continued to battle with the other-worldly beasts.

Alek gained his feet and pulled out the small dagger he kept tucked into his belt. Jess's dogs had saved him, and now he needed to help them in return. A scream came from behind Alek just before Jess lunged past him, swinging her sword in an overhead arc directed at Skilanis. The Slave Master caught her blade between his hands as it swept just shy of his chest.

"Your pets are far outmatched by mine," Skilanis sneered. "I do hope you are not very attached to them. Can you feel it? My alpha just landed a bite to one of your dog's necks. That will be difficult to survive. Still, your mutt fights on! Your pets are tenacious when it comes to your defense. I do respect that."

The look of pain and terror on Jess's face as she checked in mentally with her dogs told Alek that Skilanis was not lying. Alek threw his dagger at Skilanis's face. His aim was true, but his skill was lacking. The hilt bounced off the Slave Master's brow where Alek had hoped to bury the blade. It was not just Jess's dogs that were finding they were outmatched.

The wind kicked up behind Alek. This was no gentle breeze. It came so forcefully, both Alek and Jess turned their backs to Skilanis to see its source. Walking down the hill, and headed in their direction, was Riva. She held her hands out to her sides with her palms facing forward. The soldiers in Riva's path were blown backward or ripped from the ground altogether and thrown from the vicinity. She was a small girl, surrounded by terrifying beasts. It was unfathomable to think that kind of power was emanating from an elf as dainty as Riva. Alek thought the sight was the most beautiful thing he had ever witnessed.

CHAPTER 18

Jess turned her head back toward Skilanis in time to witness his eyes grow wide. The left side of his mouth curled up menacingly. Ignoring Jess and Alek, Skilanis walked towards Riva. Riva was still striding to meet him. As she approached Jess, Jess found it harder to stay on her feet. The windstorm Riva created was intense. Jess got down on all fours and motioned to Alek that he should do the same. There was no way the young elf would be able to hear her over the din created by Riva's hurricane-force winds. Jess pushed aside Cassidy's pain and calmly called her dogs to her. She coaxed them to stay low and crawl. With the air current so strong, the hundespor were no longer intent on battle. Instead, they did their best to simply hold their ground.

Alek reached Jess and huddled close. Jess shielded him as best she could with her body. Butch joined them in the huddle, then finally Cassidy. Cassidy was bleeding badly. Jess reached out to him and was relieved to find the source of the blood was not the dog's neck. Instead, it was actually Cassidy's shoulder that was torn open. Skilanis's pet must have thought he had torn Cassidy's throat and communicated that news to its master. Jess held Alek and the dogs tightly and pushed them as low to the ground as possible. Being blown away by the raging wind was not the only danger. The objects thrown by Riva's storm were now deadly projectiles.

Pressed this close, Alek yelled into Jess's ear, "I think it's Riva he wants! Who is her father?"

Jess reached out with her mind to the mass of unknown beasts still flying toward them. Earlier, they had still been out over the mountains to the north-west, but now they were only a few miles away. Alek's question could wait until then. Jess had been able to feel the approaching animals, but had not been able to communicate with them or direct them to act in any way. Jess suspected the approach of Riva's father was the logical explanation.

The wind relented. Jess looked up to check on Riva. The girl had not stopped her storm. Instead, her squall was now contained by the dead army. Jess couldn't see Riva or Skilanis through the horde that approached Riva's last position from every side. Every dark creature had disengaged from the smaller skirmishes spread throughout the hill and the valley to converge around the young elf. Joral, Gunnar, Bane and Frida all charged toward the area where Riva was shrouded in the enemy. Kindra and Leif disappeared from view as they teleported and reappeared at the backs of their foes. They immediately began pulling creatures out of the circle with magic and into waiting sword blades.

An ear-piercing scream split the air just as Joral and Gunnar reached the circle where Leif and Kindra were slowly lowering the numbers of the enemy. Two thuds sounded behind Jess, followed by three more. Jess turned her head toward the sounds as several more bird-like creatures landed. At first glance, Jess felt they looked like huge eagles, but then a few of the creatures turned toward the largest one in the center of the group.

"They have butts like a cat!" Alek exclaimed. "Really big cats with wings and heads like birds!"

The poor kid was excited, but at the same time Jess heard how perplexed he was. She could sympathize with Alek. Jess knew the animals before her were gryphons, but that didn't help her wrap her mind around what she was seeing. A man dismounted from the center gryphon and sprinted to the army of the dead. Each vile creature that touched the man withered where it stood and turned to dust. It was as if the man was able to pull the essence from within the beings without a thought.

"Who is that?" Alek asked Jess.

"That," she said, "is Riva's father."

"How did that work? It looks like Syndral would've died the moment he touched her," said Alek.

Jess wondered the same thing. Everything this man touched was turning to dust. *Wait; can he hear what I'm thinking? Should I stop saying he is a man? Is that offensive? Clearly, I am having trouble being in the presence of a god.*

"I don't think it works the same way it does with us," Jess answered. "I'm not sure he ever really had to touch Syndral. Vanir gods are gods of fertility. I think they can just… make it happen."

"Oh, that makes sense," Alek concluded.

If Jess could take her eyes off of the God currently cutting his way through the army of the dead as if they were nothing, she would have looked at Alek as if he were crazy. None of the last three minutes made any sense to Jess. She had just become accustomed to elves being a common presence in her life and accepted the fact that she carried their blood within her. Gryphons and gods were going to take a little adjustment.

Syndral pressed her hand to her side. The scar tissue from her wound had been stretched beyond its limit during the fighting. The pain was excruciating, but that had been Riva's scream she had heard. She had ignored the anguish the old injury caused and pushed to keep up with the others as they ran to aid Kindra and Leif, but most importantly, to help her daughter. She stopped now, allowing the pain to radiate from her side to distant points of her body, as she watched the first gryphons land.

Dreysir was running toward Riva. He sprinted to rescue the daughter he had helped to create. The daughter Syndral had begged and prayed to have as her own. Syndral fell to her knees in relief. Memories flooded her mind. She saw herself, decades younger, living in Lindel. She had been earning coin in the Dredfall Army, but dreamed of a quiet life with a family in Nalahem.

Dreysir had visited Syndral in the night. He had brought her Riva, wrapped in a blanket of wool. He had told Syndral he had named the child Riva, and she was a creation of his blood and hers. Syndral hadn't questioned it. She took the babe for her own with the promise to protect her from evil. It had not been long afterwards that Syndral understood a soldier could never be a mother while she was under the command of Dredfall's king. Syndral had sent Riva to the human realm to grow and thrive, in the same way many nobels evacuated their children during that uncertain time. The best way to protect Riva had been to give her up.

Now, with Riva having seen just over forty-three summers, Syndral was once again responsible for her protection and she had failed. Failing didn't bother Syndral as much as she expected. It didn't matter who protected her now, as long as Riva was safe. The Vanir God tearing through the army of the dead was all the security Riva needed right now.

Kindra froze as the man ran by her. A langen nearly caught her ankle as she stared after him. She stomped down on it and sliced its head from its body with a flick of Forsvarer's sharp edge. Kindra watched the man walk right into the mass of enemy soldiers, gently touching those near him. The beasts simply disintegrated. When the man reached the center of the circle of combatants, he had carved a path that allowed Kindra a clear view. She watched the man hold up a fist and roll it in the air as if he were about to throw a lasso. When he ceased the twirling motion and opened his fist, every last soldier in Skilanis's dead army fell to the ground as dust.

Tomia had told the group that Riva's father would come to defend her. Kindra surmised that this must be Dreysir. She was watching a god advance on Skilanis from behind. Skilanis watched his army fall away and dropped Riva. The girl did not move once she hit the ground. Skilanis turned slowly to face Dreysir as if he were in no rush to begin the inevitable confrontation. Kindra saw genuine fear in the eyes of the Slave Master.

"I did not think your kind deigned to interfere in the lives of those in other realms," Skilanis hissed.

The God did not bother to reply. He continued his steady advance on Skilanis, appraising the evil elf as he went.

"You are a giver of life. You do not take back that which you have given," Skilanis challenged.

Dreysir laughed. "Life is given to those who long for it. For some, it is not a conscious choice and they are not aware how badly they crave the greatest gift offered. Sometimes, removing a life offers the best chance at life for those that desire it most."

"Your twisted words are meaningless. I hold you to your agreement after the last great war of the realms. You shall not meddle in the lives of those outside of Vanaheim."

"Such hypocrisy! You've torn beings from their home realms for centuries and forced them into servitude. Don't worry. I did not kill your little pets. They have been returned to the realms from which you summoned them," Dreysir said.

"So you have not killed any being yet, but killing me will break your oath," replied Skilanis.

"I can see the future. Your plan to summon a World Destroyer from the realm of fire will leave this realm charred and uninhabitable. Alfheim will cease to exist. The being who comes to you from Muspelheim will not remain here, nor return to its own realm. Your world-ender will continue on to destroy each realm in turn once it is free to walk between worlds. I can't allow the complete destruction of life." The god sighed. "Also, your plan hinges on the death of my daughter."

Kindra watched as Dreysir finished speaking and reached out with his hand. He allowed his fingers to graze Skilanis's cheek, and Skilanis was gone. The choice to break an agreement from centuries ago was made in a second. Dreysir killed Skilanis with a simple touch. Then Dreysir turned his palm toward the sky and closed his fist.

When Riva opened her eyes, she was lying on her back and staring up at the gentle face of a man she did not recognize. The man cradled her head and helped her to a sitting position. Riva searched her surroundings. Jess and Alek were crouched down on the ground with Butch and Cassidy. Kindra and Leif stood side-by-side. Riva admired the similarities in their appearance. Just behind them were Joral, Gunnar, Bane, and Frida. Riva saw her mother on her knees. Syndral's expression showed relief, mixed with pain, as she clutched her side. They were all alive, but they were all frozen in place.

It was as if time had stopped, but that was not possible. Riva was moving. The man helping her was moving. There was a flock of eagle-like creatures behind Jess and Alek that were moving. Riva refocused on the man before her. He had sat down on the ground in front of her and appeared to be marveling over her. Riva found herself wishing she had Alek's ability to read emotion because this man looked as if he might be in awe of her.

"Are you well, my love?" the man spoke.

Riva nodded her head slowly. The man spoke as if she was supposed to know who he was. She took a breath and held it for a moment.

"Are you my…?" Riva couldn't bring herself to finish the question.

"My name is Dreysir, and yes, it is I who created you. I've eased the injury sustained when your head hit the ground. Is there pain anywhere else?"

Riva, still confused, reached her hand to the front of her skull. It came away bloody, but there was no injury. Riva looked around.

"My mother is in pain. It's her side. There is blood on one of the dogs. I can't tell if it is his blood or not," Riva said.

"Calm down, young one. I have a solution for all of that. At this moment, I am asking if you are in need of relief."

"No," said Riva. "I'm… I'm ok. Why aren't any of them moving? Well, except for the eagle things."

"Ahhhh, right," said Dreysir. "You were unconscious when I stopped time. They are not suffering in any way. I wanted to give us a moment together to speak. With regard to 'the eagle things,' as you've called them, would you care to meet them?"

Riva forced her gaping mouth shut. Tomia had said that Riva's father was a Vanir God, but somehow Riva had not grasped all that it entailed. Dreysir stood and Riva scrambled to get up. Together, they walked toward the strange animals waiting just beyond Jess and Alek.

Riva resigned herself to avoid asking about Skilanis. He was of this realm, and though Riva disliked the idea of killing anything, she did not want to think the elf had survived. As if Dreysir sensed Riva's inner conflict, he held his arm out as they approached the pride of strange animals and gestured toward them as a way to change the subject.

"These are gryphons," Dreysir explained. "They have the back legs, body and tail of a lion, but the wings, front talons and head of an eagle. The large one in the middle is Nordstern. Would you like to pet him?"

Riva reached out her hand and stroked the area where fur met feather on the creature before her. The creature turned its head toward her, cocking it in a very bird-like fashion. The animal didn't seem very happy. Riva removed her hand.

"Give her a chance, Nordstern," Dreysir soothed. "She may one day call for you and I expect you will aid her."

Riva quickly snapped her head to Dreysir's face. She felt it must have been a joke, but he showed no signs of being anything but serious. His face softened.

"You heard me correctly. I am not supposed to be in Alfheim. I will have much to answer for when I return to Vanaheim. I shall argue that my presence here was necessary to preserve all nine realms. When Yggdrasil called us to protect Alfheim, not all who sit on the council agreed we should remain neutral. I will have friends to support my claim when I return home. I do not expect it will be easy to make this journey again without more serious repercussions, so if there comes a time when you are in peril, Nordstern and her sisters will answer your call in my stead."

"Wait," Riva said. "How do I call them?"

"They will know if they are needed."

Riva was still trying to keep up. "Is Tomia really Yggdrasil? Leif said that name."

"I do not know. Yggdrasil is the tree that binds and protects the realms, both as a whole and from each other. I am sure the person called Tomia is some form or branch of Yggdrasil, but that is not for you to understand."

Riva felt flustered. This was likely the only time she would have her creator as a captive audience. She had so many questions, but she could feel that he was readying himself to leave.

"Will I ever see you again?" Riva asked.

"I don't know," Dreysir replied. "I know I will not return to Alfheim. I also know the paths of your future are plentiful at such a young age. One of those paths may lead you back to me."

Dreysir stepped up next to Nordstern. His feet left the ground, and he slowly moved his body into position above the gryphon and gently lowered himself to the animal's back.

Riva squeezed in a final question. "Why did you create me if you knew my mother was going to give me up?"

"Did she give you up?" Dreysir asked.

"She brought me to the human realm and let a human couple adopt and raise me," replied Riva.

"So you are now grown?" Dreysir asked. "Where is your mother now?"

Riva looked toward where Syndral still kneeled, frozen, on the ground, clutching her side. Syndral was here, fighting to save the realms and Riva. She had found Riva in the human realm when the risk of Riva's discovery was imminent. Syndral had sent Riva into her former enemy's castle because it meant Riva would be among people who would keep her safe. Riva bowed her head.

"That, my child, is love," said Dreysir. "You now have a lifetime to enjoy it."

CHAPTER 19

Alek blinked, and everything changed. Nothing appeared as it had a moment ago. Riva's father had pushed through the circle of enemies, turning each one he touched to dust. Alek had taken off his tunic and pressed it to Cassidy's wound. Skilanis had come into view and he was holding Riva in the same way he had held Alek a moment earlier. Skilanis had dropped Riva to the ground. Alek had been concerned that Riva may have been dead. She was slumped in an odd position and was not moving. Alek watched Riva's father reach out and touch the Slave Master's cheek. Skilanis had disappeared.

The next thing Alek saw was an open field. He turned to look behind him and saw Riva. One moment she was crumpled on the ground, and the next she was running toward him and Jess. Riva crashed to the ground next to Cassidy. The girl ran her hands over the dog, looking for wounds.

"He's ok!" Riva shouted excitedly.

Then Riva ran toward her mother. Syndral was rising from where she had fallen to her knees several hundred yards from Alek. The female warrior looked as confused as Alek felt as she stretched the muscles of her side. Syndral saw Riva running toward her, then glanced to where Riva had been on the ground. Alek felt some tension ease as he realized he was not the only one feeling as if he had missed something big. Those thoughts were washed from Alek's mind as he watched Riva throw herself into Syndral's arms for a hug. Alek had barely seen Riva smile at Syndral until now. Whatever piece of time Alek was missing, it had changed Riva immeasurably.

Alek rubbed his hands through Cassidy's fur and found that Riva's assessment had been accurate. There was no longer a wound on the dog's shoulder. Alek grabbed Jess's hand and placed it on the dog so she could feel that the wound was gone. The relief that flowed from Jess made Alek smile.

"That's not all," said Alek. "The bird-cats are gone and so is Riva's father."

Jess looked over her shoulder at the place where there had been a pride of gryphons minutes ago. There was nothing but grass. The Vanir god was missing as well. Jess stood and reached a hand down to help Alek to his feet. She pulled him up, and they made their way toward Syndral and Riva, with Butch and Cassidy beside them. Bane, Joral, Gunnar, Leif and Kindra joined them after a few hundred paces. When the group approached, Riva pulled back from the embrace she was sharing with her mother. When the girl turned to face the rest of the group, she had tears running down her face. Alek felt no sadness from the girl, however. Love and happiness flowed off of the young elf.

A female voice carried on the wind and Alek turned his head in the direction of the hill he had tried to climb earlier. At the top of the rise, Imra stood holding the reins of several horses. Alek panicked when he did not see Marbles. A hand squeezed Alek's shoulder and Alek turned to see Gunnar behind him.

"Don't worry. Marbles probably ran for Millspare. He knows the way."

The entire group traveled to Kanin's home in Smalgroth. The trip took the rest of the day because Imra had only been able to find four horses. They could only move as fast as the slowest person walked. Kanin had not yet returned, but Bane had assured everyone that it would be ok to enter the house. The group sat around the large table for Riva to share her story. When Riva had explained all that had happened from the time she opened her eyes to the time the rest of the group had ceased to be frozen, there was silence. Alek had been on edge. He had a lot of questions, but no one was talking and he didn't want to look foolish. Patience like that was far too much to ask of a young Elven boy.

"So, is Dreysir your dad or not?" Alek blurted. "I don't get it. He said he created you, but he didn't say he was your father."

It was Syndral who answered. "I don't think 'dad' is the correct word. That would imply a relationship. The word 'father' is better. Riva was created by combining genetic material from Dreysir and me, but her creation did not require any physical contact. I never carried Riva within my body. If Dreysir is not Riva's father, then I'm not sure I can call myself her mother."

Riva added, "You are my mother. You've earned that title. I suppose Dreysir earned his title today when he broke an oath to save my life."

Alek shook his head. He had little experience with family relationships. He was able to understand how a male and female could give life to a child. He had witnessed the process enough times in the dark alleys of Fallholm. The nuances and many meanings of words like 'father' and 'mother', however, were out of his reach.

That evening, Alek joined Gunnar at Frida's home. The three of them ate their evening meal together. At first, Alek was very uncomfortable. The three of them sat around the small kitchen table as they quietly ate. Frida broke the silence.

"I remember one time when your father tried to bake me a pumpkin pie," Frida said. "Gunnar here scooped out all the slimy insides and seeds from within the big fruit and mixed it up with sugar and cinnamon. He used the concoction to bake the worst pie I've ever had."

Frida laughed loudly at the conclusion of her story. Even Gunnar had to muffle a giggle. Alek looked from Frida to Gunnar. He was confused. He felt as if he had missed the funny part of the tale. Frida stopped laughing when she perceived Alek was struggling to understand the humor in the story.

"Since the pumpkins came from the human realm, Gunnar had thought he understood the process from all the time he had spent there when he was young. Unfortunately, Gunnar had prepared the pie by using the gooey parts inside the pumpkin, including the seeds. He had not realized the pie should be made from the meat of the fruit, just below the outer shell," explained Frida.

Understanding dawned on Alek and the laughter spit from his mouth uncontrollably. He could picture his warrior father trying to find his way around the kitchen and creating a pie of orange mush. Alek's laughter forced Gunnar to start laughing as well and all three of them enjoyed chuckling over Gunnar's former ignorance.

The trio spent considerable time sharing stories of their own shortcomings and misunderstandings. Listening to his newfound mother and father accept each other for who they were, including their faults, gave Alek the strength to share his own secret. Frida and Gunnar were laughing about a time Frida's leather had grown mold, when Alek had made his announcement.

"I can do more than move things with my mind. I know how people are feeling."

Frida and Gunnar stopped laughing immediately. Alek wished he hadn't said it out loud. His parents looked scared. Alek let himself absorb their emotions. Alek's power was too new to easily tell which emotions came from which person while they were all sitting so close, but Alek felt love there. It was mixed in with fear, worry, and awe, but there was still a lot of love. Frida composed herself first.

"Forgive my reaction, Alek. It is not you, I fear. I am simply trying to remember all the things I have felt in your presence, and I'm afraid I may have offended you."

The smile on Alek's face had been the most mischievous expression he ever offered to anyone. Gunnar broke out into a grin. The warrior clapped Alek on the back, nearly making Alek spit out the cake he had been nibbling on.

"Oh Frida," Gunnar said. "I fear we are in trouble with this one."

The following morning, Bane arrived at Frida's door to announce that a messenger had arrived from Gulentine through the transport portal. The entire group had been summoned to the palace. Gunnar sent the messenger on to Millspare to ease the minds of Mildred and Einar, under the guise of offering a formal battle report to Viktor and Ruth. Gunnar wrote up a battle brief for the Lord and Lady and instructed the rider to share that everyone was healthy and they would be continuing on to Gulentine. If the group was not riding for Millspare that morning, Mildred would need to know the group was intact or she might decide to ride out herself to look for them.

Alek and his parents met the rest of the group at the entrance to the transport gate. The portal before them would allow them to travel to the palace in less than ten minutes. Alek had never been through a gate before. While Gunnar had been writing his battle report, Frida had explained the portals of Lillerem to Alek. She stressed that portal travel to other realms could be dangerous for elves without strong connections to their magic, but that the transport portal was safe for everyone.

Alek's fear of the portal before him was overshadowed by his excitement about going to the palace. He stepped through the gate after Frida and found himself in a tunnel. Alek knew the other side of the tunnel was in the palace gardens. Frida had explained that this portal had been created to move produce, grown by the villagers in Smalgroth, to the king's kitchens. The light from the entrance faded and Alek took several steps into complete darkness before light started to creep in from the far side of the tunnel.

Alek stepped from the tunnel into a beautiful private retreat. The garden was walled off from the city and resembled a tiny paradise. Prymers strutted around displaying their colorful feathers, and the trees bore fruits of all colors. A mackel cat sat on the low branch of a tree, stalking one of the prymers. Its mottled coat of black and tan shone in the bright sunlight. Alek was wary of felines. He had always felt they thought themselves superior to others. The cat was robbed of its quarry when Butch bounded from the tunnel and scooped the bird up in his mouth.

"No, Butch! Drop it!" yelled Jess.

The dog placed the prymer on the ground and ducked his head. Jess must have called the dog back mentally, because Butch returned to her side looking sheepish. The prymer hopped up from the ground and fluffed its feathers. It strutted off into one of the nearby bushes. Alek swore the mackel cat rolled its eyes.

"I completely forgot how much Butch loves those birds," mumbled Jess. "I'm happy that something about this place has maintained its beauty."

Jess was looking toward the palace as she spoke. There were places where the walls were crumbling. Alek might have never visited the palace before, but he was certain the damage was new. The group followed a path to a wooden door that hung from one hinge. Bane pulled the door from its remaining fastener and leaned it against the wall. The group walked through the doorway and toward the throne room. Alek had expected there to be a lot more people bustling about. There was evidence that Gulentine had been attacked, but most of the damage in the halls the group walked through did not appear to be irreparable.

Entering through a side door, Alek took a spot next to Riva in the ruins of the throne room. King Erik was dead. His heir was dead as well. Alek was curious to know who was left among the rubble. Someone had summoned them all to the palace. There were few people around. Alek had no experience with palace life, but he imagined it had once been teeming with servants, royals, and soldiers. When Alek had stepped through the portal and into the palace garden, no one had greeted him or the others. As a group, they had walked through quiet halls of the palace to the great hall where they would have traditionally been received by the king.

There had been some damage to parts of the palace, but Alek could tell the majority of the battle and bloodshed had occurred in this room. There were no bodies, and no evidence of blood, but there were places where the white stone had crumbled from the walls and several columns had fallen. Alek found himself hoping the room was structurally sound.

Kindra stood among her friends wondering who had summoned them all to Gulentine. She thought about the only other visit she had made to the palace and hoped this vist would be less harrowing.

Trego emerged from somewhere behind the throne. He walked down the steps of the dais and joined the group standing before him on the floor. Moments later, an ancient female elf appeared. There was no mistaking Letha, the keeper of the palace archives, and Kindra was pretty sure she was wearing a pair of Ray-Ban sunglasses. Kindra thought of Krish. It made sense that he would have brought the old archivist a pair of sunglasses from the human realm to protect her vision when she ventured out of the darkness of the archives.

Krish had been a good person. Kindra had accepted that he might not have been her mate, but he belonged in this world and he should still be here to protect it. Kindra felt a definite sense of sadness over his loss, but she acknowledged that the loss was not overwhelming. It did not change the fact that Lillerem had lost its king and its heir and would shortly be in chaos, though.

"Welcome friends," Letha began. "A formal announcement will be made later today before the people of Lillerem to inform them of the demise of the King, as well as the loss of the Crown Prince. Before that denouncement, we have a few matters to digress."

Kindra had forgotten about Letha's quirk. The wise elf had a distracting habit of swapping words. She felt a little pride in herself when she was able to push it aside and continue listening to what Letha was trying to say.

"Firstly, Riva, come forward child," Letha said.

Riva took a few steps forward, stopping just before the steps to the raised platform bearing the throne of Lillerem.

"Riva of Lindell, daughter of the Vanir God Dreysir and Syndral of Lindell, knowledge of your existence and your lineage has been added to the scrolls. You are henceforth to hold the title 'Princess' in honor of your Vanir blood. One cannot defy that she who carries the blood of a god should be recognized."

Kindra was sure the word 'defy' was used in place of 'deny', this time. Once a person got used to it, it was easier to substitute in the correct words or ignore the mistakes altogether. Kindra glanced around and noticed the others, even those who had never met Letha, were doing an excellent job, looking as if they had not noticed the errors. Riva's face was the only one that evidenced any change. The girl wore a blush that made it look as if every ounce of blood in her body had rushed to the skin beneath her cheeks. Kindra couldn't stop herself from smiling as the girl stepped back into the group.

"Prince Gunnar of Millspare, please step forward," Letha said.

Looking confused, Gunnar stepped up to the spot before the stairs where Riva had previously stood.

"Prince Gunnar, as elder of this palace, and keeper of all records of Lillerem, I decree that you are now to hold the title of King of Lillerem. Please take your throne."

Letha gestured to the giant chair beside her, but Gunnar did not move.

"You've made a mistake," Gunnar said.

"I do not make mistakes," Letha replied.

The irony of Letha's reply was not lost to Kindra. Still, Kindra knew the archivist had chosen correctly. King Blaith had been the last king of the unified kingdom of Lillerem. His eldest son, Lars, had taken the throne upon Blaith's death. Lars's second son, Ulford, had betrayed the Kingdom of Lillerem and declared himself king of the northeastern portion of the kingdom. That had become the separate kingdom of Dredfall. Krish's death had ended Lars's line, and Ulford's betrayal had nullified his line of descendants. King Blaith's youngest child had been Ekkelle, mother to Ruth, Gunnar, and Leif. Gunnar, being the eldest living male child in the line, was now the King of Lillerem.

While Kindra's mind had been examining the genealogical facts that solidified Gunnar's rise to the throne, the quiet warrior had ascended the steps and was now standing with his back to his friends, staring at the large chair in front of him. Kindra noticed that one of the chair's gilded legs looked as if it had been hastily repaired. Gunnar turned slowly and lowered himself onto his new throne. Kindra was pleased to see the repair to the leg held.

Never had Kindra seen a king look more uncomfortable on a throne. Gunnar stared at the floor between his legs. Everyone in the room took a knee. There was silence as they waited for the new king to say something.

Leif spoke out of turn. "If you think this means I will be more inclined to respect your words, brother, you have some excitement in your future."

Kindra had no doubt Leif was speaking sincerely, but at the moment, his comment provided levity and there were chuckles among the group. When Gunnar still did not offer up any words, Letha stepped forward again.

"It is customary for a king to accept his position verbally," said Letha.

Gunnar looked up from his dedication to studying the floor and said, "Thank you."

"Wonderful," replied Letha. "I can't wait to record your future words of inspiration into the palace scrolls. The crown of Lillerem was recovered after the attack and is currently being cleaned. It will be ready for your official coronation. I suggest you come up with a slightly longer acceptance speech before that time."

Visions of a golden crown, bedecked in jewels and blood, ran through Kindra's mind. She pictured an elderly maid trying to scrub gore from the crevices around each stone and concluded a part of

Erik would forever travel with Gunnar. There was no way they were going to get that crown clean without bringing it to the human realm and placing it in an autoclave or something.

Letha called Alek to stand beside Gunnar. The young elf practically skipped up the steps, excited to have a part in the day's announcements. He stood on Gunnar's right side, placing his hand on his father's shoulder. Alek held his head proudly as he looked out at his new friends and family.

"Alek, you have been through much," Letha addressed the young elf. "Until recently, you were a slave of Dredfall, and an orphan. Your bravery spurred you to throw off your chains and you found your birth parents in the process. I can only imagine how you must be feeling, standing in the royal throne room of the most powerful kingdom in Alfheim. I am excited to ascend you to your rightful place in Lillerem. You, my young friend, are now Alek of Smalgroth, Crown Prince of Lillerem."

ACKNOWLEDGEMENT

This concludes the Elven Roots trilogy for the foreseeable future. Originally, the goal was to publish a single book, as inspired by my colleague, Patricia. The Elven Roots trilogy was born when my colleague, Carol, pointed out that fantasy books are supposed to be released as three, five or seven books. Since we are now at three, I feel it is time to rest. For the completion of this third installment, there are many that provided support and guidance. Some deserve to be thanked specifically.

Firstly, I need to thank my nephew, Landon. About a year ago, I asked him what his name would be if he were to become an elf. He immediately told me his name would be Alek. I asked him to describe Alek to me. What are his good and bad qualities? What is he good at and what does he enjoy doing? From there, Alek was born as Kindra's guard at the end of book 2 and then became a central character here in book 3. Of course, he earned the freckles and hair with a tendency to flop in his face from the kid who conceived the character in the first place.

A huge thank you to my alphas, betas and ARC readers. Special thanks to the ones providing the most valuable feedback. These include Niklas, Davida De La Harpe, and Raneem Abu-Nimeh, a high school student and accomplished writer. You should check out her work. My favorite so far is The Rebel's Night. Also, to Ed Cooke who truly enjoys cutting out swaths of redundant text to ensure readers remain entertained and I stay focused.

Thank you, once again, to Elena A. Steele. Her narration and production of the Finding the Past and Preserving the Present audiobooks continued to provide the character voices in my head while writing the speaking lines for Forging the Future.

Thank you to my cousin Darren for reprising his role in creating cover art for my books. I continue to be amazed by his talent. It seems as if each time I look at one of his covers, I discover a new hidden secret.

My parents, Lenore and Bob, as well as my in-laws, Millie and Willie, and my Aunt Jo Ann get my thanks for driving me to complete the conclusion of this adventure. I'm sure they will be wondering what happened with the few lose ends I've left and hoping I return to the realm of Alfheim to write more about Alek and Riva's futures. Who knows...

My husband Phil, as always, deserves thanks for being supportive when I become frustrated. Though he seems to have accepted writing as part of my weekly routine, I'd like him to know that I appreciate the time he gives up so I can do that.

Thank you to the Tappan Zee High School class of 2030. It was so exciting to see you enter grade 7 interested in my books, reading them, and asking questions about how to get into writing. Who would have thought the math teacher could be inspired by, and in turn, inspire a love of the written word for future novelists? Special thanks to Luke B. It was an amazing feeling to know you chose my novel to use for your ELA class. I keep copies of your related assignments tucked within the pages of the book I display in my home. (Yes, Mrs Stehly gave me copies.) YOU have talent, and I hope you decide to do some more writing of your own. One day, I want to be reading and reviewing your novel.

Lastly, thank you to my readers. As I am sure you know, reviews are what drive a writer to improve. Those same reviews also help sell books. Please share your thoughts about this book on Amazon, Goodreads, or your favorite social media platform. It would mean a lot to me. Keep an eye out for books to come. I really do intend to write a stand-alone fantasy or two!